D1479048

SELECTED WORKS BY JOHN CHRISTY

Hansel and Florian in the Black Forest

Bean

Fuck & Destroy

A French Book

SELECT WORK BY GENEVIEVE KNAPP

The Great American Novel Written Down Finally

THE KIDNAPPING OF MICHEL HOUELLEBECQ

THE NOVELIZATION

JOHN CHRISTY
GENEVIEVE KNAPP

© 2014 by John Christy and Genevieve Knapp
Cover and book design by Genevieve Knapp

amphetamine press

ISBN-13: 978-0615991177
ISBN-10: 0615991173

The Kidnapping of Michel Houellebecq:
The Novelization

A Note on the Title

Halfway through the writing of this book, *The Kidnapping of Michel Houellebecq* was released. The film, which stars Michel Houellebecq, has a theme similar to this novel's. The authors of this book have chosen to capitalize on Houellebecq's capitalization of himself by titling this book *The Kidnapping of Michel Houellebecq: The Novelization*. The authors humbly hope this tactic makes the book rise to the top of Google's, or at least Amazon's, search rankings, even if it, like the film, has little or no intellectual or artistic merit.

The authors have not viewed the film and do not intend to do so unless made to in court.

Introduction

In the year 2014, Google released a beta product called Google Reviews. The product had begun as a system of programs and infrastructure meant to increase the searchability and intelligence of Google Books. It created a new taxonomy of publications, in a sense, a Dewey Decimal System that for the first time in history categorized all published work in a clear, accessible, authoritative system, without human input. The system, through a precise learning mechanism, evaluated any given book's vocabulary, length, motifs, themes, structure, etc., then compared it to all Google Books' scanned work. The book then found its place in the taxonomy, and the process was complete, though every additional book changed the taxonomy by degrees. Books were assigned significance scores based on the degree that they shifted the taxonomy. The more work the system performed, the more effective it became.

During his 20% time, a Google developer integrated the system with Google's internal Natural Language Processing APIs. He wanted it to understand a user's questions and provide answers from literature. Essentially it would become a literary Dear Abby robot.

When the developer finished the integration, he emailed the new tool to the office at noon. It answered countless "What should I get for lunch?" questions with recipes from cookbooks, dietary information, and wisdom such as "I shan't begin to describe the dishes there were at the table! I'll make no reference to the cottage-cheese patties in sour cream, nor to the giblets served with the borscht, nor to the turkey with plums and raisins, nor to the dish which looked very much like boots soaked in kvass, nor to that sauce, which is the swansong of the ancient cook, the sauce served completely engulfed in flaming wine, which was very amusing and at the same time frightening for the ladies. I shan't begin to mention these dishes, because I much prefer eating them to talking about them at length." RoboAbby was a benign curiosity that was soon forgotten.

A few months later, somebody remembered the tool and, thinking that it might be more intelligent when asked about its area of expertise, requested information regarding Dan Brown's *Inferno*. RoboAbby returned the book's complete taxonomical justification, in sentences. It read like literary criticism at its finest: a massive, precise review that contextualized hundreds of elements from the book by referencing thousands of years of literature, history, and science.

With a few slight modifications in RoboAbby's method of output, Google Reviews was born. Amazon licensed the product, branded it "LitCrit," and added its review to every book's product page. A significant correlation between LitCrit's reviews and a book's success was quickly established, first in Amazon's Romance and Erotica sections. These genres, dominated by self-published authors, were outside the purview of major publications, yet they comprised Amazon's major source of eBook revenue. Year after year, unknown authors would emerge and establish immensely popular serieses. The addition of LitCrit intensified that phenomenon. It provided a heretofore unknown authority, depth, and legitimacy to the uncharted universe of these books. For the first time, readers of Erotica and Romance had a north star for their purchasing decisions. An endorsement from LitCrit meant that a book would become a mega-hit.

It wasn't long before LitCrit became the ultimate arbiter of success for all books. Some argued that Amazon gamed its own system by increasing a book's ranking and findability based on Google Reviews' internal significance scores, or, less conspiratorily, that individuals are helplessly influenceable and were ultimately doomed to emulate ideas espoused by LitCrit in their own user reviews, and, of course, in their conversations with friends and family. The accumulation of infinite quantities of these repetitive, unoriginal reviews and ideas, these critics argued, forever tainted the discourse on a book. Publishers and authors, of course, worshipped LitCrit as a prophet.

> A look through Houellebecq's eyes can permanently change
> how we view things that happen in our own lives.
> —*Los Angeles Times*

Ricky woke first. Elvia had moved away from him in the night. He could see her face slack against the pillow and her long dark hair streaming off the bed. The curves of her tight little body showed through the sheet. Ricky was hard, unlike most mornings, and he saw the opportunity he'd missed the night before.

He scooted over to spoon Elvia; in the process he got tangled in the sheets. His torso felt big and bloated pressed against Elvia's firm ass. Elvia murmured and stretched her legs. Ricky put his hand between her thighs. He wasn't sure if he wanted to stroke her or reposition her body. "Ricky . . ."

"Hold up baby," Ricky said. He began to finger her. She slid her legs up and down the mattress and softly moaned. She got wet.

Ricky felt himself begin to soften. Whatever was going to happen needed to happen now. He barely managed to push his dick inside of her. "*Chingao*, Ricky, get the fucking condom!" Elvia said. With a great effort, Ricky thrust deeper, desperate to keep himself hard, to keep going, and to fuck her like he knew he could, like he once could. He was gonna lay this bitch out.

Elvia jerked herself away from him and went searching for a condom among the trash on the floor. Ricky tried to grab her but she pushed him off. "Found one," Elvia said. She smiled, showing her chipped tooth and dimples. God, she was fresh.

"Fuck," Ricky said. His erection was completely gone. The latex would have killed it anyway.

"That's okay, baby," Elvia said. "I'll suck you off." She bent over him and took him in her mouth. She moved soft and slow, used her tongue, but the flesh didn't respond. His dick just sat there, somewhere between mashed potatoes and an oily french fry. Elvia didn't have any quit in her, but Ricky told her to stop. He couldn't take any more. It was humiliating. He thought he saw a spider in the corner. Couldn't stop looking at its dangling ass.

"Let's go get high," Ricky said. Elvia got up and began to dress. Behind her back, Ricky jumped on the mattress and smashed the spider against the wall.

They went to the old plaid couch in the living room. The morning light was weak through the glass blocks of the basement windows. "You know, it's probably them steroids you shooting up that doing this to you," Elvia said.

Ricky broke up the bud. Elvia took a book from her purse—*The Elementary Particles*. Ricky recognized the author.

"Fuck that nigga Houellebecq," Ricky said. "You still on that tip? I ain't gotta hear about it today, right, *chica?*"

"Nigga it's pronounced 'well-beck!'" Elvia said. "How many times I got to tell you?"

"French ass nigga I ain't give a fuck." Ricky made half a fist and half swung it at Elvia. He scoffed.

"You stupid, Ricky. Sitting in this basement smoking, can't see the world around you," Elvia said. She was ten years younger than Ricky but thought she had it all figured out. "You old as fuck and still chasing young cunt. That's why you like me."

"Aye, *mija*, you know it's your brains I'm after," Ricky said. "Now hit this fucking bong."

"That shit keep making you stupider, Ricky. It's all there in the book. You getting old, you scared as hell of getting weak and soft and shit, and you think you can get back your game by fucking around with young bitches."

"Scared as hell? You got a big mouth. You gonna use it to suck on this bong or what? Only reason you here is to party, ain't that right?"

"I'm trying to educate you, Ricky," Elvia said. She was getting worked up. "You nothing but a pathetic, lonely, sex needy failure. You think you running game but you just a worthless little bureaucrat, sitting your ass here dealing to bums on the block. You could be something bigger, Ricky. But you gotta learn about how the market controls our lives and culture, and religion and shit."

Ricky took a hit from the bong and held it in. "White ass Mexican," he said as he exhaled. "You smart, but you really gonna worry about the market when we sitting in this moldy ass basement? Put your head under that sink and breathe deep. When you come up I'll talk about the market."

The mold under the sink wasn't the only mold in the basement. It was just the biggest and the blackest. Ricky liked the stale, motionless basement air, and he liked that all the windows except one were made of glass blocks. It made him feel secure, and it made the biggest hotbox in the game. Smoke out the window, smoke wasted, Ricky always thought.

Elvia stood up and made like she was going to leave. Strands of hair fell over her eyes. "You real nice to me, Ricky. Real *carinoso*. Ignorant ass bitch."

Ricky stood too. "Girl, I'm not trying to fight with you over no damn book. That shit's polluting your mind. Got you all wound up and shit. Over what, some sad ass white nigga? I ran shit all over this country and made a living. Now I settle down a little, get after a steady girl, live quiet, and I gotta catch some shit like this?"

"Fuck you, Ricky. You ain't capable of love, just like Houellebecq says."

"The fuck you talking about, I ain't capable?"

"You ain't capable of shit," Elvia said, snatching her purse and phone. She popped in her ear buds and stormed out. From the only window in the basement Ricky watched Elvia's legs carry her down the sidewalk.

Ricky sat down and smoked more. He thought about going to the gym, then thought about shooting some steroids. I mean, Elvia was right that they is fucking with my dick, Ricky thought. But they were the only thing keeping his body from going to shit. He didn't pack on muscle like he did when he was twenty. Every piece of food punished him. His dick would probably come back, as long as he didn't think about it too much.

Usually there'd be people wanting to stop by, but his cell phone hadn't rung all morning. Nothing was going on today. Ricky looked for the phone anyway and saw that Elvia had left her book. "This fucking gay nigga," Ricky said to noone in particular. He picked up the book, ready to throw it out, but flipped it over and looked at the back.

"Here are ideas, here are dreams, here is a great novel," Ricky read aloud. He wondered what his own ideas and dreams would look like in a novel.

> Dream #1: Stack cash
> Corresponding idea: Run the dope game
>
> Dream #2: Have power
> Corresponding idea: Get a crew
>
> Dream #3: Get pussy
> Corresponding idea: Have dreams #1 and #2
>
> Dream #4: Make Mama proud
> Corresponding idea: Shack up with Elvia. Move to a nice neighborhood. Go to church. Get a straight job. Have kids that grow up right. Help pay off the house. Buy her a new stove. Track down my fucked up little brother. . . . Naw, fuck all that, Mama would be happy if I just called her sometimes . . .

Come to think of it, Ricky almost had all that shit back in the day. The first three, at least. He had started out on a West Side corner like everybody else. Back then he was dating Elvia's older sister. She was wild about H. When her family moved out of the city to a little town off the highway, and Ricky would drive down there to see her and hook her up, he saw an opportunity that could make him. He knew that white junkies drove all the way into the city to score. Those lames lived out here. And so did the biggest Latino-American population outside of California. Guys washing dishes at Applebee's who Ricky could make big homies.

So Ricky saved up his money, bought a few pounds of pure, and moved his game to the suburbs. He started cutting dope in Elvia's sister's bedroom and bringing it out to scared white boys in their cars. From there Ricky got big. By the time he was a direct employee of Mexico's biggest cartel, he had houses in four *barrios* for cutting and distribution, a network of apartments to sell from, and plenty of homies to handle the day-to-day.

Operating outside the city meant safety too—the cops weren't busting blocks like they did on the West Side, and the Feds were too busy trying to cut the head off the snake to fuck with the tail. But when you're six feet deep in the underworld, the pigs are the least of your worries.

"Fuck all the old shit," Ricky said. And as he said that to noone, it hurt worse that his old crew was gone. He was more alone than he'd ever been. He picked up the book just because it was still there.

"This book is principally the story of a man who lived out the greater part of his life in Western Europe," Ricky read. Don't care, he thought. "Drop that nigga in D.F. and let's see how he do," Ricky chuckled. He read on.

•

It took Ricky the rest of the day to finish the book. When he did, he was mad and confused. First, everything he'd said to Elvia was right, especially calling her a white ass Mexican for reading this shit. Really, what the fuck? What'd that bitch see in this whiny ass French nigga? If she wanted some sad tales I could've filled her in. Bitch caring about some little French boy getting a toilet brush on his face when Mexican kids are getting kidnapped, chopped up, and made slaves every day. Fuck, kids she knew got shot before they was eighteen.

Did she like the sex scenes? The bitches in the book seemed fine, but no one want to think about a wrinkly ass white nigga jerkin ill. Come to think of it, orgies and nude beaches ain't even real. That's the straight bullshit they sell you in porn.

Ricky thought about a dude he used to know who swam in pussy. That nigga worked at a club and had the finest *llello* money could buy. He sure never went on an online sex site, and he sure as fuck never beat his own self off on the train like the niggas in the book did.

Maybe Ricky just didn't get the book because all the shit about societal molecules and shit didn't seem like part of the story. Those fucked up white boys getting old and sad—that's what Elvia was always saying was happening to him. Wow. That cunt had some nerve. Maybe she want her uterus scooped out like the bitch in the book, or she scared of turning into some fucked up hippie whore in a wheelchair throwing herself down a staircase. Ain't no one he knew fucked with shit like that—that was some white people shit.

When Ricky's dad got old and sick, the nigga kept his head up. When he couldn't get around anymore, the family took care of him. Ricky's mom and sister fed the nigga, dressed his ass, even changed TV channels for the nigga. And why should he lose his pride and start feeling guilty? Pretty fucking common for your daughter to take care of your old ass. I mean, the shit was expected of them. And Ricky's sister—fuck, she wasn't ready to have no goddamn baby—sure as fuck didn't leave the kid to go fucking dudes in a commune and sitting in funny poses. Shit may have changed in "Western Europe," but that don't mean shit to the rest of the world and people living their lives.

Elvia would probably abandon their kid. Or abort it. If he managed to knock her up.

That seemed absolutely true to Ricky.

It was cause of this nigga Houellebecq. Ricky knew that Houellebecq wasn't the nigga directly responsible for Elvia being fucked up, but still, it rang true that it was Houellebecq's fault. He, and the niggas he writes about, will be responsible when Elvia's a fucked up old single lady with nobody to lean on. Elvia might have been right that the market, or the system, or what the fuck ever controls peoples lives, but the bitch didn't realize that the nigga telling her about that shit was the nigga repping the whole thing. Houellebecq was taking away Elvia's family, starting with Ricky.

•

Over the next few days, Ricky shot steroids, worked out, and made a few deals, but all he thought about was Houellebecq and Elvia. He didn't text or call her, but he knew she'd be back. She was a fiend for weed, just like her sister was for H.

Ricky heard a gentle knock at the door and knew it was Elvia. "It's open," he shouted. For some reason he grabbed the book. When she walked in he shoved it at her. After a confused pause, he said, "You left this."

"Relax, Ricky, I'm not here for that." She smiled and put her hand on his shoulder. "What you been up to?" She kissed him lightly.

"I read the Houellebecq," Ricky said.

She sort of giggled. "I'm sorry about that shit, Ricky. I know you ain't give a fuck about that, and I never meant to fight with you."

Ricky stepped away from her and sat on the couch. He'd meant to talk to her about the book, tell her everything she didn't get about the way shit is, but now that she was here he didn't have shit to say. She seemed weird somehow. Part of him wanted her to go away.

"What's up with you, Ricky? Acting all quiet." Elvia followed him to the couch. "Usually I get here and you wanna tell me all about the nigga on the block with the blue shirt who ask you for dope everyday and never got the money. That nigga still standing at the fence hollering for you?"

"Feeling like my head's messed up or something."

"I got a cure for that, baby. Let's get high and fuck. I'm horny."

"Uh huh," Ricky said.

"Alright, baby. I'ma go pee." Elvia plopped her shit on the coffee table and skipped out of the room.

Ricky looked at the mold on the wall where Elvia had been standing. On the table her phone buzzed and lit up. Ricky blinked and ignored it. The second time it vibrated, it got his attention. He looked down and saw an email notification.

From: Joshua Larson
Subject: Whoops, forgot to attach the poem. (:

Ricky grabbed the phone, entered Elvia's passcode, and tapped the notification.

"Earth City"
Earth is full of cycles:
Revolutions and rotations,
Cinders and conflagrations,
Nomads and nations.
Some dress themselves in armor like skulls,
Reinforcing the effects of causation.

Out in the forest,
In out on the town,
You can find that everything
Tends to move around.
Minds are full of questions.
To aggravate or pacify?
Acquiesce or challenge why?
Do the best or just slip by?
Some answers change because they are lessons.
People perceive, and reality replies.
Where belief persists,
Truth will be found.
So where wrong is seen as viable,

Truth just goes around.
If All is seen as right and good,
Unhappy makes no sense.
If all are simply understood,
Truth engenders progress.
Love transforms causation through perspective.
If no one attacks, armor is not needed.
Exposed minds see an other as self-reflective,
The nature of the whole as endlessly connective,
The notion of an enemy as foolishly deceptive.
So the cycle of division is defected.

What you think is all you could
Chokes on coins of speculators
And blindly hinders all you should,
If you do not see the paradox of systems.

Hope transforms ideals through actions.
If everyone hopes together, cooperation is unremitting.
Circling the whole becomes the goal of each transaction.
Fiery hearts depolarize to douse the flames of factions.
Exclusive flags unify to forge inclusive satisfaction.
So living all in harmony, here we are in Earth City.

It's from a nigga named Joshua. He sent this. To Elvia. And there's more, because the nigga forgot to attach this shit to whatever else he sent. Ricky was somewhat stunned. He hit "Inbox." There it was.

My dear joyful spirit,

First of all, thank you for such an incredible message. Discovering that in my inbox sent a buzzing grin through me, deep beyond my face.

Though I certainly didn't fret it, I felt a tinge of sadness when I learned you had already left on Saturday, so it is nice to know that it occurred to you too.

You are right; there is SO much more to say! I can barely believe I am still up right now, given work tomorrow, but I couldn't wait any longer to write you back.

I watched the Alan Wallace lecture last night; it is truly phenomenal. While I'd prefer to save most comments for in-person dialogue, a couple notes:

- Have you read *The Universe in a Single Atom: The Convergence of Science and Spirituality* by the Dalai Lama? I recently read it, and you would love it if you don't already. In that book, he also calls for the first revolution in the mind sciences, though framed in his own way, of course.
- I LOVE how Wallace just rocks out that argument for

epistemic pluralism. Step by step, in the most simple language, he exposes the parallel between modern and ancient prejudices.

- I LOVE "after all, we are the ones who define physical; nature didn't define it for us."

I know very little about Alan Watts; I will check out the lectures you recommended and report back.

And now, I leave you with a poem of mine from a few years ago, which is of course riddled with my own academic disciplines, but nonetheless talking about the same stuff. It's attached.

lovepeacehappinessinfinity (lphi),

Joshua Adam Larson

Elvia came out of the bathroom wrapped in a towel. Ricky was frozen holding her phone. He hadn't even heard her start the shower.

"Hey," Elvia said. "You snooping in my personal shit now? What you looking at, Ricky?" She padded over and took the phone from Ricky's hand. "Oh! Joshua wrote me!" Elvia sat down, pressed her body to Ricky's, and eagerly read the message. "I didn't know the Dalai Lama wrote a book," she said.

Ricky sat there not looking at her or thinking anything. The words, "That's how college boys get pussy," flashed in his head. "Did Joshua show you Houellebecq?"

"God, shut the fuck up about Houellebecq, Ricky. I came here to fuck so come off it," Elvia said.

"Did Joshua show you Houellebecq?"

"What's your problem? He shows me lots of shit. Not like you."

"You know that nigga just want to fuck you."

Elvia's eyebrows shot up. "You got a lot of nerve, Ricky," she said slowly. "And you ain't got no friends. You don't know what a friend is."

Ricky smiled, but it felt more like a sneer. For the first time he saw Elvia as deeply, truly stupid. She wasn't worth arguing with. "Yeah, another thing I ain't capable of, I guess."

"What the fuck you talking about, Ricky?"

He picked a nugget of weed off the table and started to break it up. The tiny green scraps fell into the bowl. Ricky made sure each piece was packed neatly in place. Clutching her phone, Elvia waited for something to happen.

"Oh, you still mad at me about that shit from the other day?" she offered.

Ricky hit the bowl and leaned back.

"You tripping, Ricky," Elvia said. She pursed her lips and looked at him. He blew the smoke into the living room. "Stupid ass nigga, I'm out of here."

Elvia got up and stood over Ricky. She was still clearly waiting for him to say or do something, but it was like he didn't see her. She went to the bathroom to retrieve her clothes. "Okay, I'm out, Ricky." She dropped the towel and slowly pulled on her jeans. She hopped around, pretending to struggle to pull the tight cloth over her ass. She looked up and smiled, expecting Ricky to be looking at her. He wasn't.

Her top went on with less fanfare. "Your head's fucked up," she said, looking genuinely disgusted. "I ain't coming back, you know that." She opened the door and made to leave. As she stood at the threshold, she said, "You driving me out just like my sister."

Ricky grabbed the bong and smashed it on the coffee table. Glass and brown water went everywhere. Elvia shielded her face with her arm. "Get the fuck out," Ricky said. He knew she was gone when he heard the door click. He sat there letting his hand bleed onto the couch.

Ricky couldn't remember everything Joshua's email said. He knew it was all repulsive. The only part he remembered said "thank you for your message," meaning that Elvia had written to Joshua first. Ricky thought he would like to see what she wrote. No, he would rather stuff his bloody fist down his own throat.

> Gloom suffuses the works of celebrated French
> novelist Houellebecq.
> —*Booklist*

Houellebecq was looking for Doritos. He stood in front of a display stuffed with snack bags. He'd been there for five minutes now, standing, looking, considering. The *Chino* at this corner usually had Cooler Ranch and Nacho Cheesier, but today the Cooler Ranch had been replaced with Sabritas. Houellebecq reached for a bag of Nacho Cheesier, but let his hand drop. He was back to considering. The best you could get in Spain was Cooler Ranch and Nacho Cheesier. At the moment, Houellebecq would have liked Chilli Heatwave, but he would have also accepted Spicy Nacho or Taco. He'd ordered those flavors online before, along with a host of others. He knew he could only get them online, but now that his second choice wasn't available (fourth, or even fifth choice really), he wouldn't settle for what felt like no choice at all.

The illusion of consumer choice carries the average person through a meaningless daily existence in what could be deemed a pleasant, even pleasurable, state of mind. But was it really an illusion—there has got to at least be one Spicy Nacho flavor nestled among the rows of Nacho Cheesier. The manufacturer could have made a mistake and shipped a single bag of Spicy Nacho among the Nacho Cheesier bags, which had a similar color scheme. Spicy Nacho was only a slight shade redder.

Houellebecq pulled bags of Nacho Cheesier from the shelf one by one, inspecting each, front and back, for about 30 seconds. He cradled a pile of rejected Doritos which grew ever larger until it became unmanageable. Houellebecq caught a falling bag with his free hand and was surprised to find himself with his arms completely full. Was that a different bag in the back?

All the Doritos tumbled to the floor. The Chinese cashier, who had been reading a paper, looked up. Houellebecq's body was blocking the view of the snack stand. "*¿Que paso, señor?*" the cashier said.

"*Que se rompió, perdón*," Houellebecq muttered and left the store.

He stormed past a tall man reading a newspaper and made his way through the streets at a quicker pace than usual. Once home—a modest apartment that he'd bought cheap in the nineties—he regretted not buying that bag of Nacho Cheesier.

He considered trying another *chino*, but he was exhausted. He fed his dog, crawled into bed, and nibbled bits of stale bread and mortadella. It was two in the afternoon. He fell asleep mentally composing a polemic against the Chinese, against Doritos, against everything.

•

The tall, skinny man who had observed the spectacle in the *chino* had been following Houellebecq for three days. He'd learned that he didn't have to hide himself. Houellebecq lived a bit like a farm animal.

Criminal Graves, as he liked to be called, ate a can of spaghetti while he watched Houellebecq sleep on his truck's big monitor. This was the boringest assignment he'd done in a while. He couldn't even imagine it getting more interesting once he kidnapped Houellebecq. What was the guy gonna do—smoke cigarettes between bouts of weeping?

A police cruiser pulled up in front of Houellebecq's house. Ah, things were finally starting. In a few minutes, that cop would arrive at Houellebecq's door, take off his hat, and tell Houellebecq that his mother had been murdered.

•

The pounding on the door woke Houellebecq. He pretended to continue sleeping. The pounding continued. It occurred to Houellebecq that it was something like two p.m., and it was completely implausible that he'd be asleep. He continued the charade. The dog started barking. When Houellebecq realized that no one could see him pretending to sleep, he opened his eyes. He was still undecided about answering the door. If the knocking went on, the person out there really cared about him.

The knocking seemed to have stopped. Houellebecq threw the sheets off and dashed to the door. He always slept clothed.

He opened the door and saw a female police officer waiting for the elevator. She turned around. "*Señor* Houellebecq?"

"*Sí?*"

She took off her hat. "I have sad news. Can I enter?"

Houellebecq showed her to the kitchen and gave her a glass of water.

"Pardon that my English is not so good and I do not speak French," she said. "I am from the local precinct on behalf of the French embassy. I am here to tell you that your mother was murdered in her home on the island of La Reunion."

"Murdered? She is more than eighty years old." The scene wasn't playing out the way Houellebecq had always imagined it.

"There are not details yet. I am sorry for your loss." The officer set the water on the table. "Would you like me to stay with you?"

Houellebecq wondered if this was a come-on. Maybe it was standard procedure. "You can leave," he said. He searched for a cigarette. She left, quietly closing the door.

Houellebecq sat at the table and drank the rest of the officer's water. He had written about his mother's death before, and in those scenes he never felt much. Now that it actually happened, he felt like something had been taken from him. Maybe it was the possibility that she could love him, love him enough to apologize for abandoning him. He wondered if her book sales would improve. Maybe her book would finally be translated into English. And what about his own sales . . .

The situation called for a moment of tenderness. Houellebecq looked for his dog. He found Clement in the bedroom, chewing on a wrapped condom. Houellebecq turned away in disgust, as much at Clement as at himself for never having used the condom.

Houellebecq returned to his bed and lit a cigarette. He lay in bed smoking and thinking. Suddenly he leapt up and dashed to his writing room, the flat's second bedroom.

Houellebecq always kept the writing room's shutters closed. This required him to wade through total darkness to find his desk—a journey that seemed worthwhile in theory but proved to be nothing but terrifying and pointless. He opened his laptop and squinted at its blinding square of light.

Houellebecq wrote, "Could God make a woman so perfect that even she could love Him?"

He slammed the laptop shut and trod back to bed. It wasn't long before he nodded off.

•

Houellebecq woke at eight in the morning, which meant that he'd slept for almost 20 hours. He was angry for not having slept into the afternoon. Then he remembered that he had a meeting at nine with his agent. He grumbled, got out of bed, slipped into his fuzzy slippers, and walked out the door. He hoped Clement could walk and feed himself. After all, Houellebecq, a critically acclaimed author, still had to somehow.

It was ten degrees, a cold day for Spain. Houellebecq had luckily fallen asleep in a hoodie and thick woolen pants. He shambled down the street. The shopkeepers were out, hosing down the sidewalks. He hadn't been up early enough to see that in a while. His fuzzies were getting wet. Fuck.

In the café, he ordered an aperitif, though he didn't plan to eat. Maybe if Bill ordered, Houellebecq would eat out of politeness. A potato. Of course he didn't have any material for Bill. This Spanish holiday had been unproductive. He had no ideas. Maybe he was finished writing altogether. *Le Carte et Le Territoire* may very well have been his last novel. He had already eroded the foundations of contemporary culture and thought as much as he was able.

He would tell Bill all that, but mention that he suspected that writers often said that they were 'giving up writing' and never meant it. Bill was used to dealing with writers. They vow never to write again, only to sneak off and write their magnum opus, don't they? That's why Houellebecq would tell Bill that at all costs, Houellebecq could not go on book tours or engage in publicity stunts. He wasn't writing, didn't plan to, but just might.

Come to think of it, he had written something. Something about God and a woman. It was just a scrap. If he remembered correctly, it was, "Could God make a woman so perfect that even she could love Him?" Maybe it was meant to be a koan.

> Clement asked Michel Houellebecq, "Could God make a woman so perfect that even she could love Him?"
>
> Michel Houellebecq took out his penis.

It took Houellebecq 40 minutes to solve his own koan. He wondered if koans had market appeal. The market itself may be a koan, Houellebecq thought. Now we were getting somewhere. This completely changes the meeting with Bill. Come to think of it—where was Bill?

It was 10:15. Houellebecq found a pay phone and dialed the agency's number. When he asked for Bill Jim, the secretary fell silent for a moment. "I'm sorry. Who's calling?" she said.

"This is Michel Houellebecq."

"Mr. Houellebecq, sorry to be the one to have to tell you. Bill is dead. We found out this morning. Some sort of accident, some lunatic broke into his place. The police are questioning everybody here. We're all in shock.

"Of course, we will assign you another agent of your choice at the earliest convenience. If you want, I—"

"I will call back later."

"Is there a number at which we can reach you?"

Houellebecq hung up. So, they got to Bill too, Houellebecq caught himself thinking, though he knew the death of his mother couldn't possibly have anything to do with Bill's death. He headed home, somewhat sorry that he couldn't share the koan. He would certainly forget it now. He would have forgotten it as soon as he told it to Bill anyway.

•

Criminal Graves checked his watch. He had expected Houellebecq to call the agency after fifteen minutes, twenty at most, but the old fool had sat for hours with a constipated expression. The way Houellebecq was, Graves could have just left a note on the table that said that Bill Jim had died.

Complex jobs were almost never this monotonous. Even tax accountants had more going on than this "writer." At any rate, the first steps were over. Houellebecq's mother, agent, and friend Beigbeder had been killed. There was nobody else whom he'd contacted in the last year. A hooker, but she couldn't identify him, nor would she care to. Now Graves needed to pay Houellebecq a visit.

•

Houellebecq returned home. Through his flat's door, he could hear Clement whimpering. That meant Clement must not have given in and pissed on the floor. Probably the dog held it so he could get that walk, Houellebecq thought.

Houellebecq opened the door and took Clement's leash from its peg. Clement's whimpers turned immediately to excited yips. He wagged his fat little tail. A Corgi is really a ridiculous animal—stunted to the point of debilitation, ignoble, and excitable. When Clement lay on his tummy, pressing against the cool floor, his legs were too tiny to tuck up or stretch comfortably; instead they occupied their own tiny irrational spaces, like nuggets. Houellebecq had always found this quality particularly endearing.

Before Houellebecq could attach the leash, Clement bounded out the door and down the stairs. Houellebecq sighed. He had just purchased matching fluffy bunner slippers for Clement, and he fully intended to outfit the dog with them before they went out. Houellebecq grabbed the bunners and dashed after the dog.

When Houellebecq got to the stairwell, he heard a strange thud. He tiptoed down the stairs, his heart pounding. Halfway down he peered into the lobby. He couldn't see much—the lobby's tinted windows turned the brilliant Mediterranean sun into a network of shadows. Houellebecq's eyes wandered over the double doors and the rows of mail slots. "Clement?" he whispered. He heard movement from the back of the lobby, which he couldn't see. In the middle of the marble floor, there was a chunk of whitish hair. Houellebecq recognized part of Clement's tail.

Houellebecq ran up the stairs and toward his apartment. He stopped short at the door he'd left open—had he heard footsteps behind him? If somebody was coming for him, they'd look in his apartment first. He ducked into a neighbor's doorway.

Houellebecq breathed slowly and silently. Was this some kind of Arab revenge plot? No way could women conspire against me, Houellebecq thought. Would Clement ever get to wear his fluffy bunners? He heard the footsteps coming up the stairs.

•

Houellebecq had been out of Criminal Graves's sight for far too long. On the kitchen surveillance, Graves had seen Houellebecq grab the leash and doggy slippers and let the dog out. That would have given Houellebecq and the dog 45 seconds to a minute to get out of the building. But they never came out. Maybe the old man slipped in the stairwell.

Graves drummed his fingers on the dashboard. Houellebecq was starting to bug him. If he took it in his head to commit suicide now or had a little accident for attention and landed himself in the hospital, Graves wouldn't be able to finish the job and get paid. That would make two weeks of wasted time and a pile of pointless stiffs.

This is as good a time as any to pick Houellebecq up, Graves thought, even though the idiot hadn't yet received the news about Beigbeder's death. Graves hopped out of the van and crossed the street to Houellebecq's building. The street was perfectly empty. No way did Houellebecq sneak past him. When Graves got to the building's door he saw that the lock had been smashed open. Rarely did Graves feel panic or even concern, but he did now. Houellebecq was never supposed to be in real danger. Maybe there was more to this job than what Graves knew. He'd have to have a little talk with his client. Graves pushed the door open.

What was left of the dog wasn't pretty. Its neck had been broken and the attacker had chopped at its torso a few times. The dog had vomited. Bits of Doritos swam in its blood.

Graves flattened himself to the wall and took out his gun. He inched along the lobby wall, headed for the staircase. If Houellebecq made it through this, Graves would tell him to feed his next dog better.

Graves heard scuffling upstairs. He peeked up the staircase and pointed his gun, hoping he didn't have to blast whoever came down—that would bring a lot of heat on Houellebecq's building. He saw Houellebecq. The old man was sweating and tottering faster than Graves thought he was able. Somebody was behind Houellebecq. Graves ducked out of sight.

"I'm gonna kill your French ass, nigga!" the man shouted.

Houellebecq made it to the lobby. When he saw Clement's body, he squealed and collapsed.

"Mister Houellebecq, I'm here to help you," Graves whispered. "You have to come with me as soon as possible. Your life is in danger."

"Those filthy Arabs!" Houellebecq wailed.

Graves crouched and prepared himself for a fight. The American who was after Houellebecq was barreling down the stairs three at a time. When Graves saw the axe in the air, he whirled around and slammed the butt of his gun where he knew the guy's jaw would be. The guy dropped cold, tumbling over Houellebecq.

Houellebecq screamed and closed his eyes, cradling Clement. "Scum! The Muslims think they can do this to me without inciting the hatred of the world! What else will their God permit?"

Graves pulled the balaclava off Houellebecq's attacker. He was a puffy, baby-faced Mexican covered in bad tattoos. The word DOPE ran up his neck in a floral script. How did something like this ever get shipped out of the States?

"Mister Houellebecq, I'm Jack Reacher, an agent with the Centro Nacional de Inteligencia. I was sent to protect you from a dangerous killer," Graves said. He hesitated. The clown on the floor looked anything but dangerous. "From a lunatic. A lunatic is after you." Graves flashed his badge and tucked his wallet back into the inner pocket of his jacket. He hadn't expected to be giving this speech with a dead dog and a knocked out Latino in the room.

"You need to come with me right away," Graves said. He took Houellebecq by the arm and gently lifted him to his feet. The dog's body tumbled out of Houellebecq's arms. They walked toward the van. Graves would have to make Houellebecq call building maintenance and explain that there'd been some sort of accident with a stray.

·

Crossing the street with Houellebecq on his arm, Graves tried to make sense of what had happened. He would have liked to have picked up the attacker—in fact, leaving him might blow his cover. What kind of an agent hit somebody and left instead of taking him in for questioning? But there may have been a second hit man upstairs, and Graves couldn't risk Houellebecq running off if Graves had taken the time to go after the second guy. Moreover, Graves didn't know if his own client had hired the men. Better to keep Houellebecq safe now and ask questions later.

"Some imam has issued a fatwa against me, hasn't he?" Houellebecq murmured. His French accent made him difficult to understand.

"I'm going to need whatever information you have," Graves said. "We'll talk once I get you to a safe location."

Graves drove Houellebecq across town to the small flat Graves had rented for the kidnapping. All in all, taking in Houellebecq had been much easier than Graves had expected. The sudden appearance of that Mexican was incredibly convenient. Graves had been worried that Houellebecq wouldn't feel threatened by the murders of his mother, agent and friend, wouldn't be convinced that he was in danger, or, worse, would resist going with 'the authorities' for his 'safety' because he would rather die. But Houellebecq had been terrified. He had obeyed without question.

They sat in the kitchen at a small table, the only furnishing in the room. Houellebecq asked for a cigarette. "I'll have an agent bring you some. It's not safe for you on the outside anymore," Graves said. "At least until we figure out who's behind all this. I have some questions for you."

"Go ahead. I do not know anything," Houellebecq said. "All I know is that an Arab killed my dog this afternoon. I saw his tan skin and dark hair!"

"Do you have any connections to the Mexican mafia? The cartels?" Graves said.

Houellebecq laughed. "I knew cops were idiots, but this takes the cake."

"Do you have any reason to believe that anybody wants you dead?"

"I already told you—the Arabs! I said some nasty things about them in an interview once. I wrote that I hope a lot of them die. And I mean it, as much as I mean anything," Houellebecq said. He looked suspiciously around the room. "What became of that man after we left? You should have arrested and interrogated him."

"In a high-risk situation, every second is a gamble you take with your life," Graves said. He paused, waiting for a retort, but that answer seemed to satisfy Houellebecq. "Do you owe anybody money?" Graves ventured.

"No, but my publisher owes me money," Houellebecq said.

Graves sighed. He wasn't getting anything out of Houellebecq. He hoped his client had some answers. "Well, Mister Houellebecq, we have reason to believe that the man who attacked you today is connected to the deaths of your mother and your agent. We've had you under surveillance for some time now, but weren't sure anything was going to happen."

"Impossible. Nobody knows where I live."

"If you think that you can hide in Western Europe, you're a fool," Graves said. "Now here's the plan. You'll stay here with me tonight while we wait for your new identification to arrive. With your new paperwork, you'll take a plane to the United States—nobody will look for you there, knowing that the great writer Houellebecq has categorically refused to go there."

"But I have already visited California."

"Well, shit. That's not what the report said. Even an intelligence agency can't know everything. Anyway, once you get to the States you'll await instructions. We'll alert you when it is safe to return."

"If you are going to all this trouble, send me to Thailand. If I am going to cooperate, I would like to enjoy myself."

"These are my orders. The plane ticket was bought long ago. I don't get to decide, and neither do you. I have to make some calls to let the agency know that you're here and you're safe. Get some rest. You'll find clothes in the bedroom," Graves said. "Change your shirt. There's dog blood on it."

"What if I will not cooperate?" Houellebecq said.

"You don't have to do anything you don't want to do, Mister Houellebecq. I saved you from an axe-wielding maniac today. Think about it," Graves said.

"If I do cooperate," Houellebecq said, crossing his legs and shaking his foot, "what assurance do I have that I will be safe?"

"There are no assurances in this world or the next," Graves said. I've talked enough, Graves thought. He had to get his client on the phone and get some answers. Graves left the flat and barred the door behind him. Houellebecq couldn't break down that door, though Graves didn't expect him to try.

Back in his van, Graves switched the monitors from Houellebecq's apartment to the hideout flat. Houellebecq was sitting at the table with his fingers in Clement's fluffy bunner slippers, walking them along the table. Graves kept one eye on Houellebecq while he activated a new disposable phone. He called Tim, the American who'd given him the job. Tim answered right away.

"Fuck you," Graves said. "The writer job's a bust. I'm gonna plug him and leave him in a ditch."

"Whoa, whoa, calm down, brother. What the fuck are you talking about?" Tim said.

"The job was supposed to be clean. Who ordered a hit on the writer? Who's gonna pay me for putting down that amateur? Or are you getting paid to conduct a little show?"

"Don't get your panties in a bunch, Graves. You know I don't double deal."

"Then it's the client. He has two hours to explain the Mexican or I plug the writer and disappear."

"Mexican? Hold on, Graves. The client is a creep, some kind of rich faggot from California or something, but he was specific about the job. This job ain't like nothing we ever done before, you know that. I don't know nothing about no Mexican," Tim said. "Hang on, the guy only talks on chat, he's online twenty-four seven. I can talk to him, but you ain't gonna like the answers he gives."

"Just read them to me straight."

"Alright, Graves, I've got him right here. See? Calm down. Now what do you wanna ask?"

Graves thought about it. The guy who'd gone after Houellebecq was close to useless. Houellebecq was basically a stiff, one foot in the grave, a breeze could have knocked him off. It might not be a problem to keep him safe—but it wasn't part of the job. "I want more money. There's a hit out on Houellebecq. I don't care who ordered it, but I get two days on my bodyguard fee for protecting him."

"One second. Let's see . . . " Graves could hear Tim tapping on a keyboard. "He says, 'MICHEL HOUELLEBECQ CREATES THE MOST PERFECT ART. YOU ARE PRIVILEGED TO GIVE YOUR LIFE TO PROTECT HIS.' Now Graves, I told you you're not gonna like it . . . Tell you what, I'll pay your fee, come on, the creep's dropping a lot of cash on this job."

Graves smacked the phone on the dashboard. Tim's voice came through, far away and tinny. "You still there? He's typing more . . . Shit, you're not gonna like this. You want to hear it?" Graves put the phone on speaker. "BOOKS ARE THE CARRIERS OF CIVILIZATION. MICHEL HOUELLEBECQ CARRIES THE WESTERN WORLD ON HIS MIGHTY SHOULDERS."

Graves was convinced of three things: 1) Tim wasn't shitting him, 2) the maniac hadn't ordered the hit, and 3) there wasn't any information to get out of these idiots.

"You're taking jobs from nutcases, Tim, and I'm the one getting cracked," Graves said. "Tell him that when I drop Houellebecq at the airport, I'm done with him. If an axe-slinging Mexican is waiting for him, he's going to have to give the Western World a break. I swap the dental records, plant the stiff, bomb the place that day and get paid, game over. And I'm going to collect the extra from you."

"Yeah, yeah, no problem with the extra. Just finish the damn job and make it convincing. He's still typing, you wanna hear it?"

Graves hung up. The worst part of this job was its utter futility. It was absurd to imagine that you could wipe out every trace of somebody's identity and they couldn't just get it back by walking into a social security office, consulate, or whatever. Graves sighed deeply. He looked at the monitor. Houellebecq had fallen asleep in his chair at the kitchen table.

Houellebecq pushes notions of hope and hopelessness to a dismal and logical conclusion.

—*The Economist*

Ricky came to with his jaw throbbing. He rubbed his chin and opened his mouth. That caused a piercing pain, but at least the bones weren't loose in his head. Had that nigga, he thought. What the fuck. Did he trip and fall? Naw, he saw some big gangly motherfucker at the last second. Big old white bastard. Ricky never saw noone creeping around Houellebecq—but what the fuck did he know. Rich people hired bodyguards all the time.

Ricky pulled himself to his feet and caught a glimpse of his reflection in the glass double doors. He was covered with the dog's blood, which was drying to a burnt color. Can't walk around looking like this, he thought. Can't even go back to the hostel. He shouldn't have killed that damn dog. It gave everything away. But he couldn't help it—he hated dogs, little parasites. You think you own that dog? Ricky thought. Naw, that dog owns you. You live around that motherfucker, not the other way around. Get stuck doing all sorts of bitch shit. All these hard niggas in the hood on their hands and knees scooping up poops. And Houellebecq's dog was a goddamn freak. Stumpy ass leg motherfucker, turd body ass motherfucker. Can't even respect a dog looking like that.

But the smallest, stupidest looking dogs had the sharpest teeth. Ricky had learned that from a chihuahua in the hood. Turd body was coming straight at me—I did what I had to do, Ricky thought.

Figuring that he accidentally did Houellebecq a favor by killing the dog, Ricky was more determined than ever to kill Houellebecq. Where did that motherfucker go? Ricky would clean himself off, ditch this messy axe, head back here when the dog's cleaned up, and wait for Houellebecq to come back. Maybe Ricky would kill Houellebecq with his bare hands. Ricky was encouraged by the fact that he'd never had his prints taken in Spain or anywhere else in Europe. He was clean and outside the system.

Ricky headed for the beach. Houellebecq lived a three minute walk away. That was specially enraging. Where Ricky lived, you had to take two buses to get to the beach.

By the time Ricky reached the sand, the dog's blood had completely dried. Something still felt squishy as he walked. He sat down in the sand and checked his right shoe—there was something fuzzy stuck to its bottom. He took the shoe off and whacked it in the sand until the fuzzy bit flew off. Ricky crawled to see what it was. He didn't have anything better to do.

He found a twig in the sand and broke it in half, creating a sort of chopsticks. Fumbling a little, he used them to pick up the fuzzy thing.

One side was pink. He could see veins. The other had a fine fur. It came to a point on one end. Must have been the dog's ear. "Fuck!" Ricky shouted. He threw the ear at the sand as hard as he could. It hit with the fur side down and slid along the sand.

Ricky picked up a handful of sand and threw it at the ear. Then he cupped his hands, filled them with sand, and gently deposited the sand on the ear. Though all he could see was a mound of sand, he still felt the veins in the ear to be present. He kicked away the sand until the veins were back. He could hide the ear by putting it in his mouth . . . He picked it up and put it in his pocket. He put the twig in his mouth instead. It seemed that he could taste the dog's blood.

There was no way to find Houellebecq. He probably wouldn't return to his apartment. Ricky chewed on the twig and sat in the sand. Another failure. A more simple failure than the ones that landed him on his ass in a moldy basement on the West Side. Once a bitch, always a bitch, Ricky thought.

The twig was turning into sawdust in Ricky's mouth. Looking along the beach, he saw a dilapidated playground. A Spanish kid was giggling on the swingset. His mom was pushing him. Her hands looked like Godzilla paws. The dad was standing off to the side taking pictures. He was long and soft, with greasy, curly hair and a giraffe neck. Ricky had expected Spaniards to look like Mexicans. None did, except maybe the fat old men in fedoras who Ricky had seen standing at street corners and smoking cigars. Even they looked more like movie Mexicans. Ricky instinctually hated them and every western European he had seen so far. He hated them the same way he hated the white businessmen and tourists in downtown Chicago.

The kid fell out of the swing and started crying. It occurred to Ricky that these people were the Conquistadors. These were the niggas who wiped out Ricky's native ancestors, took them for slaves, or fucked them. Now Ricky spoke their language.

Ricky lumbered over to the playground. He wasn't sure what he was gonna do. When he crunched on the gravel they all turned to look at him. Fuck you niggas, Ricky thought. They went on staring while he reached up, grabbed a straight bar above him, and pulled himself up. He had gotten weaker. He struggled, but when he let himself down he pulled up again, kicking his legs and throwing his head back to finish the rep. He saw a flash of the sky. It had a cloud in it that looked like a tit. Motivation. He repeated the motion, struggling all the more, just to get a glimpse of that sky. Now it looked like a brontosaurus was licking that damn titty. He pulled up again, propelling his body toward the all-inviting sky, hoping to see a fat pussy up there. Instead he saw a dog. Houellebecq's dog. He lunged for it, feeling like his biceps were tearing off his body. He was jealous of the dog. He'd like to be able to make somebody lose his shit on sight like the dog made him. He kicked as hard as he could and jerked his head back to get his chin over the bar. Bathed in sweat and gasping for breath, he dropped to the ground.

He raised his head and saw that the Spaniards had left. The beach was desolate, a uniform tan surface with a strip of blue. He imagined it in the summer, filled with people, probably white people. Definitely white people. White ass Italians, white ass Spaniards, white ass British and Germans, all with their big old white bodies, sunburnt ass flaking skin, salty hair, holding iPhones and tablets, making business deals, playing in the water. They were happy, sipping expensive coffee, talking about sushi and urban farming, thinking they saving the world. If the world ever ended, that's probably how it would look, Ricky thought.

They ain't belong here, Ricky said to himself.

I am brown, Ricky said. From the equator. I am in total fusion with this beach, down with the sand, losing my gangsta in the waves of the water. And the white niggas, however rich they may be, can never buy themselves the body they want to see on this beach. My skin drinks the sun, and I was born in the dirt.

Ricky made his way to the water. He waded in and scrubbed his face and arms with sand and water. It was freezing. Time to head back to the West Side.

A sharp check on [Houellebecq's] hubris
—The Wall Street Journal

Houellebecq stared out the window of Jack Reacher's van. Riding in somebody else's vehicle always made him feel like a child. All there was to do was sit there and let things come to pass.

Reacher tossed a huge stack of documents on Houellebecq's lap. "You've got everything you need in there to hide out for as long as you need, the rest of your life even," Reacher said. "Passport, Spanish Visa, French IDs, an American birth certificate and Social Security card, bank account, credit card, cell phone. You're a new man, Eddie. Dual-citizen too."

Houellebecq glanced at the packet then continued looking out the window. The Spanish countryside zoomed by. Houellebecq wondered if he'd ever see the scrubby little olive trees again. "Eddie," he said. "And the surname?"

"Michaels."

"Edward Michaels. And what about my accent?"

"Nobody ever bothers with that. You're American born, raised in France. Something like that. Needless to say, you can't access your bank accounts, credit cards, personal records, and things of that nature. You won't be able to, in any case."

"What?"

"The people who are after you are very sophisticated. They can and do monitor everything—the moment you log into a bank account, they have your location. After all, it's only temporary, until they're behind bars. You can vent your frustrations when you testify against them."

"I will never go to court again," Houellebecq said. "I had enough having to listen to those fucking liberals whine about the Arabs' fundamental humanity. As Foucault said, society can exist only by means of the work it does on itself and on its institutions. And I, Michel Houellebecq—"

"Eddie Michaels," Reacher interrupted.

"I refuse to work on behalf of the judicial institution to perpetuate what you call society."

"What I call society you wouldn't like to see." Reacher smiled at Houellebecq.

Houellebecq could hear the slightest bit of accent in Agent Reacher's speech. He wondered if he was from some American or German backwoods. Houellebecq wanted to ask what was in the back of the van, behind the black cage, but he realized he was a little scared of Agent Reacher. For the rest of the ride, Houellebecq chain smoked.

At the airport, Reacher bypassed the parking lot and drove straight to the terminal. He reached across Houellebecq's chest and popped open the passenger door. "You can go. Your plane ticket is with your other documents."

Houellebecq made no motion to leave. "You are not coming with me? What if this 'murderous killer' is waiting for me in the airport?"

"The airport is crawling with CNI agents. Your safety is assured. Besides, nobody knows you're here. Eddie's ticket was purchased months ago."

"You act as if I am a nobody. Do you realize that I am famous? People recognize me. I have to avoid the public. I take private flights."

Reacher looked sceptical. "Mister Houellebecq, I've followed you for longer than I would've cared to, and the only being I ever saw recognize you was your dog. Even then I had my doubts . . . Those bored, overfed eyes . . . my God . . . In any case I've cut your hair."

Houellebecq touched his head. Sure enough, he felt stubble rather than the choked-out weeds that had been growing there. "Mister Reacher, I will have you know that my hair was a source of joy. To you it may have seemed unkempt, but to me I enjoyed fluffing it out to accentuate my aged appearance."

A man in a reflective vest blew a whistle and gesticulated at the van. "That's your cue to leave," Reacher said.

Houellebecq stepped out. Reacher pulled the passenger door shut and started the van. The radio played something cinematic. Houellebecq knocked on the van's window. "What will I do when I am in America?" he shouted over the din of an airplane taking off.

Reacher rolled down the window. "You wait," he shouted. The van peeled out of the terminal. Houellebecq headed inside.

•

It was two hours until the flight. Houellebecq wondered if he should get on the plane. It seemed just as good to stay in this airport, drinking from the stainless-steel fountains, crapping in the stalls, sleeping on the stain-proof carpet, and so on. He could learn to love the big jets and their habits, knowing their arrivals and departures, the particular sounds of their engines (certainly different planes sounded different). The only thing that worried him was those purported CNI agents. Would the thugs try to shove him on to the flight? Perhaps if he stayed in the airport an agent would befriend him, sneaking heart-to-hearts when no one was looking, but for the most part staying away, watching and protecting—only Houellebecq would know he was there. Of course that agent would have a personal life, separate from the airport, with a woman and children, and so on. How could he devote himself in full to Houellebecq?

What if he was a female agent? A beautiful, black female agent? Houellebecq began to weep. Sobbing openly, he approached the ticket counter and dropped the documents on the desk. The woman behind the counter didn't look up. "Ticket and passport please."

"It is all there, everything."

She scowled and flipped through the packet. Probably she takes me for a retard, Houellebecq thought. Well, let her. I will not remove the passport and ticket for her. A hopeless man can not cooperate! "I am Michel Houellebecq," he muttered.

"Excuse me? Everything is ready for you, Mister Michaels. If you have no luggage, please proceed to gate G."

Looking desperately into her eyes, Houellebecq asked if she read books. "Not today, sir," she said. She looked past Houellebecq and chirped, "Next!"

Now they are going to touch me with those wands, Houellebecq thought, half gleeful and half filled with despair. But the security guard waved him through the detector without any fanfare. Houellebecq touched his sleeve. "I have an item," he said.

"Place it on the belt," the guard said.

Houellebecq stepped back through the detector and placed his prescription pill bottle of Xanax on the conveyor. "My medication," he said to the woman at the X-ray machine. The little amber bottle tumbled through the rubber flaps.

"You must place it in a plastic bin," the woman said. She waited for the bottle to pass through the machine, grabbed it, and handed it back to Houellebecq. He put it in the bin of the person behind him. The guy gave him a dirty look but allowed the bin to pass through the machine. As Houellebecq stepped through the detector again, he caught a glimpse of the little white pill circles on the X-ray monitor.

This back-and-forth with the security personnel was the most contact with strangers that Houellebecq had had in months. These sorts of interactions always reinforced his distance from other people and left him feeling more attached to himself than ever. He found the gate and sat down. He began to sing one of his poems.

The dominion of machines will then be complete
And pure information will triumph and fill

A little girl who had been sitting nearby moved to a different row. Houellebecq watched her. She sat in her seat and bounced up and down. Houellebecq closed his eyes. There was a strong cheese stink coming from the food court.

The empty carcass of the empty divide;
And this noise will rule until the end of time.

He opened his eyes. The girl was gone. Everyone around him was looking at phones or computers. Houellebecq opened the phone that Reacher had given him. It was the cheapest model of phone, no frills, just a keypad and a small, durable screen. He wondered if it was possible to play a game on this thing. He hadn't had a cell phone in years and had no idea how to go about finding a game. Perhaps he could speak into it. "Game," Houellebecq said.

The little girl had returned. She stood nearby and looked at him. "I know a game," she said. She was carrying a small box of pizza.

"Where did you get that pizza?" Houellebecq asked.

"Don't you want to know about the game?"

"How is it that you know English?" Houellebecq asked.

"Susan, come here," her mother shouted from somewhere behind Houellebecq. The girl darted away.

Houellebecq got up and headed for the food court. The smell of cheese got stronger. It was coming from Pizza Hut. Houellebecq found space in the crowd gathered there. He saw a conveyor belt in the back where a man waited for tiny pizzas to roll out of the oven. The moment a pizza was within arm's reach, the man snatched it and dropped it into an appropriately tiny cardboard box, which he efficiently folded shut. Another pizza man waited to transport the boxes to a heated display. One by one, at lightning speed, he shoved the boxes onto the display shelves. Everyone was gathered around the display. As soon as a new pizza was added, someone grabbed it and hustled to a cashier. The people jockeyed for position, subtly shoving each other and craning their heads to see what the pizza men were doing. Every now and then, when a pepperoni hit the display and was snatched, the crowd grew anxious, fearing perhaps that no more pepperonis would emerge. The same could not be said for cheese.

It was not lunch or supper time, the other food stalls were deserted, and once people obtained their pizzas they did not rush to return to a particular gate. There was no apparent cause for this pizza craze. Here in this corporate pizza den, demand far outstripped supply. Yet economists point at Communist bread lines as an example of non-market systems leading to gross inefficiencies. Who could argue that Pizza Hut was not a rational economic actor? There is no market model that can account for a sudden, overwhelming human desire for Pizza Hut tiny pizzas. Houellebecq went on to compare this irrational pizza frenzy to the unpredictable nature of the boom-and-bust cycle in market economies, or, perhaps, the Dutch tulip mania, and he was thinking of the fact that tulips were themselves edible when he remembered that he was now Eddie Michaels. These sophisticated thoughts were cut off to him. What would Eddie think?

Pepperoni. Houellebecq pushed to the front of the crowd, setting off a chorus of protests. Just then a pepperoni and something called a "Sausage Supreme" slid to the front of the display. Houellebecq hesitated, trying to decide, but the hand that reached for the pepperoni caused him to grab both pizzas. He too was capable of competing for resources. He carried the pizzas to a cashier, enjoying the jeers of the crowd. With a touch of pride, he handed over Edward Michaels's credit card. The cashier offered the receipt for him to sign. Houellebecq signed his name and left the counter.

He made it back to his seat before he realized he was supposed to sign as Edward Michaels. He could dash back to Pizza Hut in an attempt to retrieve the receipt and correct the signature, but he didn't have enough time. The plane was already boarding. He tucked one Pizza Hut box under each arm and prepared his boarding pass and ID to show the attendant. He was sweating, thinking about that receipt. Would a bank even honor the transaction? He had no experience with such things. In any case, he would enjoy the pizzas.

Houellebecq found his seat. It was an aisle seat. He cursed. He wanted to open a pizza but was worried that the stranger who had the window seat would be big and fat and unable to get past Houellebecq without knocking the pizza to the floor. Houellebecq stared down at the tiny red hat that represented Pizza Hut and waited. The cheese would be getting cold soon. There was a man loudly talking a few aisles down. "Some nigga got the nerve to bring some stank ass Pizza Hut on this plane."

Houellebecq thought again of the receipt. The cashiers probably didn't dump the drawer for another hour, so if anyone found that receipt, Houellebecq would already be halfway to New York.

A fat American businessman squeezed by. As he passed, the man eyed the Pizza Hut with what was clearly naked desire. Houellebecq instinctually placed his arms over the cardboard boxes. The captain began his spiel. Blah blah, the weather, the time in New York. Houellebecq began to nibble. He'd save the pepperoni for last. The plane wound around the runway and began to take off. The sausage supreme had a special type of thick, sticky grease that both pooled on top of the cheese and coated the crust. This, more than the beaches, prostitutes, or Clement, will be my presiding memory of Spain, Houellebecq thought.

The fatass took out his devices. IPhone, tablet, laptop, Kindle. All were organized in a semi-circle on the pull-down dining table. The man plugged his earbuds into the tablet and wedged the buds over his chubby earlobes. The laptop came open. Music began to blare from the earbuds. The man logged onto the Internet and pulled up a news site. He flicked his finger such that headlines and images raced across the screen at a dizzying pace. "LeBron James Fitted for Facemask." "You Won't Believe This Simple Way to Put Yourself in a Coma." "Egyptian Army Ridiculed After 'AIDS Detector' Video Goes Viral." Houellebecq chuckled at that one. "France's 'Enfant Terrible' of Literature Michel Houellebecq Blown to Smithereens." Houellebecq choked on his Pizza Hut. The man flicked some more. "Substitute Teacher, 72, Arrested for Furiously Masturbating in School Hallway."

Houellebecq grabbed the fat man's forearm. "Excuse me. Can you please show me that one?" He pointed at the screen. The fat man looked at him with horror and pulled the earbuds off of his head.

"What?"

"That one. Click it please."

The fat man jabbed his finger at the screen. An article came up explaining that the 72 year old man still "had it," "it" ostensibly being libido and the ability to reach climax. "No, no, the one about the *enfant terrible*."

Grunting and shaking his head, the man swiped back and poked the screen. The article showed a picture of Houellebecq's Spanish high-rise with dark smoke pouring out of the second floor window. An entire chunk of the building was lying on the sidewalk. The article explained that a charred corpse had been found in the second-floor apartment. Dental records had identified 58-year-old Michel Houellebecq. An Islamic terror group with ties to Spain had come forward and taken responsibility for the bombing, claiming it had fulfilled a long-standing fatwa against the controversial writer. These reports could not be confirmed. No others were injured in the bombing.

"Seen enough?" the fat man said, reinstalling his earbuds and turning the laptop away from Houellebecq.

Houellebecq pulled the man's earbuds out. "I am Michel Houellebecq," he said.

"Michel who?"

"Michel Houellebecq! The man in the article!"

"Sure, buddy." The fat man put his earbuds back in and ostentatiously increased the volume on his tablet.

"My teeth are soft and decaying. I am the only man with such teeth—how could they have mistakenly matched my dental records to a stranger's?"

The man acted like he hadn't heard.

Houellebecq stood up. "I am Michel Houellebecq, you idiot! The famous writer! I have been known as France's *enfant terrible* for as long as I have written!" The man jammed the button that summoned the flight attendant. "No! Look at me. Look at the portrait in the article! Do I look like a dead man to you?"

The flight attendant was an acne-ridden Polish fatface. "Is there a problem, sir?"

"I am not dead!"

"Of course you aren't, sir." Her lipstick gleamed in the sick light of the plane's cabin.

"I refuse to be dead!"

"Sir, do you have medication on this plane?"

"Yes . . ." Houellebecq pulled the Xanax from his pocket. "This is for my anxiety. Some people take it recreationally. Would you like some?"

"I understand that many people get anxious on flights."

"You do not understand. I have just read an article that stated—"

"I'll bring you a complimentary Coca Cola so that you can wash down your medicine."

Houellebecq sat down and began to think very strange thoughts. If the Arab who had killed his agent and mother had been responsible for the bombing, he would have never falsified a stranger's dental records—he would have wanted to kill the real Houellebecq. Perhaps the Arab was a failure who just wanted to trick his master. If so, what guarantee would the Arab have that the real Houellebecq wouldn't emerge? In fact, how would the Arab know that he, the real Houellebecq, was in hiding with a fake identification? Could the Arab have considered the involvement of Jack Reacher's intelligence agency? On the contrary, this could be simple police incompetence. They found a charred body in his apartment and wrote it off as Houellebecq, without actually bothering to cross-reference the dental records. Houellebecq had heard stories like that—it was all too easy for the media to buy a lazy statement from the police, particularly given Houellebecq's fame and reclusiveness. When Houellebecq would later emerge in the public eye, it would delight everybody. As soon as he arrived in New York, he'd take a plane directly back to Europe, to France maybe, and announce to everyone that they were wrong. Michel Houellebecq was triumphantly alive.

The attendant returned with the Coca Cola. Houellebecq swallowed three Xanax. As he began to doze, he realized that he'd never participated in international intrigues, only gently considered them over cigarettes. This was something new.

•

Houellebecq woke with his ears popping. The airplane had begun to descend. He must have been out for five or six hours. The fat businessman next to him had been replaced by a dark-skinned ethnic with a lot of tattoos. This man seemed more bloated than fat. He was eating Houellebecq's pepperoni Pizza Hut. "Bitch nigga ass Houellebecq. You finally opened them old eyes."

Houellebecq's elation at being recognized was instantly dampered by the realization that this might be the next episode in the saga of crimes perpetrated against him. For this man definitely was no admirer of his work—it was doubtful whether he could even read. Houellebecq wished he had a cigarette. "You are eating my food."

"I got hungry." The man looked away from Houellebecq and fell silent.

No killer would behave in this manner. No gun for hire would touch my Pizza Hut, even for a moment, Houellebecq thought. Certainly this was nothing more than an overgrown, wretched specimen of American life. Just some lowlife they swapped in when the fat businessman requested another seat.

The runway came into view, and before long the airplane's wheels slammed against the asphalt.

·

Ricky had watched Houellebecq sleep for six hours, thinking the whole time that it would be easy to smother him with an airplane pillow. They always knocked off old niggas that way. But Ricky thought there was a chance he could get away clean if he just waited until Houellebecq hit up a bathroom in the airport. There was no plan any more, just determination to get the job done. Ricky didn't have long to wait now.

He knew it was sloppy to be sitting next to Houellebecq. It was even sloppier to eat his pizza and talk to him. But Ricky wasn't going to let the nigga out of his sights. If that bitchass bodyguard had been around, he wouldn't have let Ricky get close, and he wouldn't have let Houellebecq screech and whine to the whole plane. God gave Ricky a second chance at Houellebecq by putting them on the same plane. The Almighty had never helped Ricky out a whole lot, and Ricky wasn't about to let Him down when His will so clearly wanted Houellebecq dead.

Houellebecq was a bitch. Nigga sat there and let Ricky eat his pizza. Not even the pussiest ass nigga in the hood would let someone take their cookies like that. Not even a woman. Why did Elvia think a nigga like this had something to say to her? What did this whiteboy have to say about a proud Latina's life?

The stewardess told everybody they could exit. Houellebecq popped up right away. He must have been scared after all. Ricky dogged his heels, but everyone else stood up and yanked luggage from the overhead bins. Houellebecq got trapped between a duffel bag, a rolling suitcase, and two 17-year-old girls. They were wearing baseball caps, chewing gum, and pulling their shorts out of their crotches.

Houellebecq moved close to them. His nose neared their shoulders. "Get a move on, nigga," Ricky said. "Jailbait sniffing ass."

"Jailbait?" Houellebecq muttered.

"Yea nigga, that pussy cost you fifteen years in the pen." The girls looked at Ricky with disgust. "Put some pants on, hos, it cold as hell outside," Ricky said.

Houellebecq squeezed past the girls and Ricky followed close. The pair made their way into the airport. "Where you headed?" Ricky asked.

"I am going back to Europe, where I belong. I will not step foot in this fat, wretched country."

Ricky wondered why Houellebecq was on the plane. It didn't matter, he just had to ice this nigga as soon as possible. "Don't you got to pee?"

"Why are you talking to me?" Houellebecq said. "For your information, I have had nothing to drink for the past twelve hours but a sip of Coca Cola."

Ricky pushed Houellebecq toward the men's room. "Let's go, nigga," Ricky said. Houellebecq loudly protested. But they were already in the bathroom. Ricky took Houellebecq to the stall in the back. There was a father and his six-year-old son at the urinals.

"I want to go in the toilet," the kid squeaked. Ricky would have to keep Houellebecq quiet until these two left.

"Grown-up boys go in the urinal, Skylar."

Ricky had one hand on Houellebecq's mouth and the other around his neck. "Keep quiet, nigga," he whispered. Houellebecq made grunting sounds.

"Daddy, why did those two men go to the bathroom together?"

"Some types of men . . . Some types of men go to public bathrooms together to help each other feel good."

Houellebecq weakly pushed against Ricky's chest. He jerked his head to the side and shouted, "Help me! I am not a homosexual!"

"Sorry, my son is here. I can't help right now . . . I'm not gay either, I get it. Let's go, Skylar." Ricky and Houellebecq heard their footsteps leaving, and the man whispered, "I'll keep watch outside, don't worry!"

Ricky wrapped his hands around Houellebecq's neck and squeezed. Houellebecq's eyes began to bulge. It took longer than Ricky had thought to choke somebody out. While Ricky squeezed he focused on the grime between the mismatched tiles. Killing this bald-headed old nigga wasn't nearly the redemption Ricky had imagined. It was more like capping a stranger on the street for no reason, and at least when you did it with a bullet it was over in a second. Ricky's grip loosened for a moment and Houellebecq gasped. "Why," Houellebecq choked, "did you kill . . . my mother?"

"What, nigga? I didn't kill noone's moms. I'm killing you nigga!" Ricky wanted Houellebecq to shut up. He had to get this over with and book it.

He began to choke Houellebecq again, harder, but Houellebecq managed to squeak, "The cunt, I hated her! You did me a favor! But why my dog!"

Ricky put Houellebecq in a headlock and started punching the back of his head and kneeing him in the ribs. Houellebecq fought desperately, biting Ricky's forearm and drawing blood. That dog had fucked everything up. Houellebecq should have shit his pants when he saw Ricky, but after all, Ricky was just a washed-up drug dealer on a crazy revenge tip. Even this stiff old whiteboy could smell it. Ricky was pathetic.

He threw Houellebecq against the bathroom wall. Houellebecq's head cracked a tile. He fell to the floor with a thud and lay there with bloodshot eyes, gasping and moaning, with Ricky's blood running from his mouth. "I am dead already. Have you not seen the news?"

Ricky put his hands on his knees and caught his breath. He left the stall and slammed the stall door. The queer with the kid was waiting for him next to the drinking fountain. "Ohh . . . That sounded rough. Where's your friend?"

"What, you want a turn?"

The man giggled. "I can't leave Skylar alone."

"I'll watch the kid," Ricky said. "Fuck his ass up. He'll let you do anything."

"Language, language," the man said, shaking his finger at Ricky and beaming at Skylar. The man went into the bathroom. Ricky wondered if Houellebecq would lie there and take it.

"What is dad doing?" Skylar asked.

"Chill on it, little man," Ricky said. He snickered, thinking about Houellebecq taking it in the ass. He wandered over to a newsstand and looked at its candy selection. Raisinets are some old bullshit, he thought. Whoppers . . . Now that's my shit . . . Six bucks for that little ass bag? Fuck that! Ricky started looking at the books. Skylar snuck up behind him. "Mister, mister, can you get me Raisinets?"

"Raisinets? Fuck that, little bro. We can share some Whoppers if you promise not to grow up like your daddy."

"I'm never gonna grow up!"

"That gets you half of one malty milky ball," Ricky said, laughing. He set the bag on the counter. Next to the register was a stack of *New York Times* newspapers. On the front page Ricky saw Houellebecq's apartment building in Spain with black smoke shooting out the second floor. "FAMOUS AUTHOR MICHEL HOUELLEBECQ MURDERED IN EXPLOSION."

Ricky bought the issue and stuffed it under his arm. "Come on, we'll go see what your old man's doing," he said, grabbing Skylar's hand. They ran to the bathroom.

The pervert was whispering and grunting. "Playing hard to get, huh?" Ricky kicked the stall door open. Houellebecq, fully clothed, was standing in front of the pervert, who was jerking himself off. Houellebecq watched in a trance, like he was seeing rims spin for the first time. Skylar screamed.

"Let's go, motherfucker, you coming with me to Chicago," Ricky said. "You ain't gonna bring me down with some bitchass setup." He grabbed Houellebecq and dragged him away from the faggot.

·

This fat, retarded American of questionable ethnicity was clearly the same repulsive individual who had murdered Clement. None of Jack Reacher's associates had arrested this degenerate after the disastrous scuffle in the lobby, and no undercover agents had recognized and apprehended him in the Spanish airport. It was hard to say that there had been a single agent in the airport. Houellebecq wondered if that was run-of-the-mill government incompetence or if there was a larger conspiracy afoot.

Either way, Europe felt far away. Houellebecq was thankful that he had not been raped by an airport homosexual, but even that may have been preferable to whatever was to come. The fat thug jabbed Houellebecq's shoulder, ushering him toward another gate. "Unhand me, ruffian," Houellebecq said.

"Ruffian? This ain't old English, nigga," the ruffian said.

"I will cooperate with whatever you want, so long as you remove your monkey hands from my person."

"Monkey? Hell no, nigga." The ruffian slapped Houellebecq on the head.

"I am not a nigger," Houellebecq said.

"Of course you ain't. You might be a faggot though. Faggot ass nigga."

"I am not a homosexual, and I am not a nigger. I have no desire to involve the police—your useless, militarized law enforcement apparatus—in my life, but you must realize that you are kidnapping a man of international interest, and that you will not get away with this."

"I ain't know what you just said, nigga, but the law ain't gonna help your ass bust my ass, cause the minute I see a badge I'm popping both of us."

They arrived at a ticket desk. "My friend here needs a seat on flight 237 to O'Hare," the ruffian said.

"Okay, one moment . . . There are seats available. Would you prefer to sit together?"

"Yeah. I got a ticket so put him next to me. Seat 5A."

"Okay. Seat 5B. That will be $561.34 with tax."

"Go on, pay the lady."

"You beat me up, abduct me, and you expect me to pay the way?"

"Nothing in life is free, nigga." The ruffian smiled at the attendant.

Houellebecq paid. He was sure he could break free of the ruffian and make a dash for it, maybe get past a security checkpoint and get a plane back to Europe, but the fight in him was fading. He could summon no will to struggle. In some sense, he had always wanted to be part of some dark drama. In one of his books, a pervert who fancies art—intensely—steals a dubiously valuable painting of Houellebecq's, then kills Houellebecq—God knows why—perhaps for the pleasure of cutting apart Houellebecq's body with a special 21st century medical instrument, making long ribbons and quivering globs out of all parts of Houellebecq, then arranging the parts in some sort of elaborate mandala—the centerpiece: Houellebecq's own testicles. When Houellebecq thought about what this ruffian could possibly want, and what could possibly be in Chicago, he could only conclude that it had to be part of a grand scheme—violent criminals, beautiful women, and plenty of intrigue.

The attendant handed Houellebecq the ticket. He and the ruffian went to the seating area to wait for their plane. They sat beside one another in awkward silence. "So . . . ," Houellebecq began after some time, "you are a powerful man, then?"

"Fuck yeah I'm powerful," the ruffian said, flexing and pointing at his puffy bicep.

"I see." Neither said anything more.

•

Just as the the plane landed in Chicago, Ricky dropped the newspaper in Houellebecq's lap. Houellebecq glanced at it and threw it back at Ricky. "Yes, you fool, I told you in the bathroom that I am dead. Some corpse they found in my apartment has been identified as me. Are you now going to explain what this all means?"

"What nigga? When I caught you up at JFK you said you were in a rush back to Europe. A nigga sees a headline like this and gets to thinking that you were sliming back to the old country to tell a story about the guy who killed your dog and busted up your place. A hard nigga like that is real enough to bring the boom boom on your building."

"You profess to have nothing to do with this?"

"You the nigga who professing innocent. I told you I killed pups."

Both thought that over while pushing through the Mexicans, fat white women, and big shouldered bros who were inching through the airport toward the train that went into the city. Once Houellebecq and Ricky reached the station, a filthy utilitarian space with concrete and glass tiles, they broke free of the crowd and stood at the far end of the platform.

Ricky put his hand in his pocket and found the package of Whoppers he'd bought with Skylar. He ripped it open and started tossing Whoppers in the air and tracking them down with his mouth. Houellebecq studied a large cardboard advertisement. It showed a black man who had been branded on his face. "Burned by Menthol Cigarettes," Houellebecq read out loud. "I am surprised these advertisements are prolific in your country, since your country purports to offer personal freedoms."

"You get a loose square for fifty cent," Ricky said. "On the streets," he added.

They looked at each other suspiciously, neither sure he had understood. A train pulled into the station. "Where are you taking me?" Houellebecq said. "Why are you taking me anywhere?"

"I'ma tour you round the West Side, nigga. We get to know each other, know what I mean?" Ricky said.

"I have never swam with the small fry. You will bring me to the man in charge of you, and the others important in these dealings."

Ricky laughed. "Only Ricky's in charge of Ricky."

"Ricky, if that is your real name, you are clearly not telling me the whole truth. Why would you target a world renowned author except at the behest of some international criminal enterprise? I am curious to meet these men, given that they entrusted such an important mission to the likes of you."

Ricky studied the little old nigga who stood in front of him. "Man, what the fuck you talking about? I was gonna pop your ass cause you write a bunch of old bullshit that I ain't like. Your dog was my bad, I freaked out, nigga, old stub-legs got up in my face. But all this shit about the criminal enterprise, man, them days been over. For a while, know what I mean?"

"You do not have to lie to me. I am already cooperating with you without the assistance of a happy illusion," Houellebecq said. "In a way, all of this action has come at a crucial juncture in my life. This could be considered a rejuvenation to my career. My writing has been finished, I have no friends or peers, and there is nothing new to anticipate but death; the conclusion of my life was going to be a grey beach. Now, with your help, I will enter a new phase . . . Houellebecq's American period, the biographers might call it. All I need from you is an introduction to your criminal milieu. You can then leave me to my own devices."

The train opened its doors. As they stepped aboard, Ricky thought that if Houellebecq were to show up anywhere on the West Side, the cops would pick him up in a second. If Houellebecq had money, the cops would take him in for trying to buy drugs, and if he was clean they'd take him in for tossing the drugs he'd definitely just bought. That's assuming he don't get rolled first and go crying to the cops himself. Then he'd finger Ricky.

Neither Ricky nor Houellebecq wanted to sit beside the other, so they took facing seats across the aisle. "Alright, nigga, I'll show you the ghetto. But you stick by my side so you don't get fucked with. Aite?" Ricky said.

"So now you are offering your services as my bodyguard?" Houellebecq asked sourly.

"Hell no. I'ma make sure that you only see what I want you to see, because you only gonna write what I want you to write. I came for you because you the great white writer, and if you gonna poke my hood with your pen, I'ma make sure you do it right."

"You will not interfere with my creative process," Houellebecq said, crossing his legs. "You will not so much as see a word I write."

"This ain't a partnership, nigga. If you step out of line you gonna be a random victim of gang violence."

Houellebecq looked at the people on the train. Nobody so much as glanced at him or Ricky. Everyone wore earbuds and hunched over a smartphone. "You will kill me before I allow you to touch my manuscripts."

"You act like them pathetic ass sex scenes is sacred."

"So you are familiar with my work after all," Houellebecq said. "I cannot write without the utmost level of privacy. And regardless of how it appears to you, my work is a harmoniously orchestrated interplay of acts and ideas; even a stranger quietly reading my work will introduce an irreparable discord in the manner it proceeds."

This nigga gonna put me to sleep, Ricky thought and closed his eyes. "I ain't going to sleep," he announced. He tilted his head against the plastic behind him and tried to imagine the near future. First order of business was getting blazed. Man, it'd been forever. Ricky needed to get a bit of relaxation in his system. Gonna be pretty hard to kick it with this scrawny jackal creeping around. Ricky wondered if Houellebecq smoked. Hell no. It takes a strung out nigga to be spitting that shit in *The Elementary Particles*.

"Hey, you into speed?" Ricky asked.

"Meaning a stimulant?" Houellebecq said.

"Yeah nigga. Ups," Ricky said, adding a hiss to the s.

"A friend once gave me an Adderall. I wanted to try it for writing. Before I sat down to write I thought I would comb my dog; you see, he had been running in the meadows and accumulated a quantity of cockleburs on his underside. I began to comb, delicately removing the plants from the dog's fur. This activity consumed me.

"Clement was patient, but the drug had made me more patient than he. After three hours he began to squirm, then he broke free of my hold. I followed and observed him wandering about the house. I was in a state of agitation, feverishly thinking about the dog's comings and goings, until finally I took Xanax and went to sleep.

"My beloved Clement . . . Thank you for killing him so swiftly," Houellebecq said. "I cannot bear to see animals suffer."

"You shoulda told your big old bodyguard about not liking them suffering animals. My face been sore since he put me down."

"That man was not my bodyguard."

"Who the fuck he was then, nigga?"

"He worked for the Spanish intelligence service."

Ricky laughed. "Nigga . . . Ain't no cop in the world drop a nigga to the floor and leave him to take a nap. Ain't no cop knock someone out like that, period. Nigga woulda shot or tased me if he was popo."

"Then who do you suppose he was?"

"Fuck if I know. Why don't you call his ass up?"

Houellebecq scratched his face.

"What's wrong, nigga, he ain't leave you a card?" Ricky began to laugh. "You better phone the precinct then, nigga. You might find him up your butt nigga. Hahaha."

The train was pulling up to Chicago Avenue. "This our stop," Ricky said. They stepped off the train into a dingy underground station. Water was dripping from the ceiling. "Smells stank as hell down here," Ricky said. "Must be raining." Houellebecq fixed his attention on a busted up umbrella. That nigga always looking at shit that ain't worth seeing, Ricky thought.

"So this is the American metro," Houellebecq said.

"This ain't shit," Ricky said. Houellebecq seemed kinda funny or messed up. He was annoying as fuck, but maybe the nigga wouldn't be too bad now that Ricky was back to his old digs. Now all that Ricky needed to make shit feel right was to hit the bowl.

They climbed the blue-painted stairs and emerged in the weak light of a cloudy spring day. "So this is the American ghetto," Houellebecq said, taking in a white glazed building with a pink "Gelato!" sign, a large convenience store, a gallery with spindly furniture in its windows, and a multiracial crowd of teenagers flooding out of a drama school. "What a diverse city."

"Fuck nigga, this ain't the ghetto. Them kids you see is rich fags. Thems is thirteen years old sucking on each other's dicks and pretending to be Shakespeare . . . Nah nigga, the kids in the ghetto is black and Latino. And they straight. This shit . . . Right here it's rich. We hit up that bus and you get a close-up of the hood."

Houellebecq looked at the kids. "The girl children . . . They are very ugly."

"The fuck you expect, nigga? They pimple face fatties. You getting on this bus or what?"

"They are fatter and plainer than one would expect. Are these the ones who are fed corn?"

"Corn, nigga?" The bus was pulling up. "Let's go. Damn," Ricky said. Houellebecq was still staring, so Ricky grabbed his arm and dragged him on to the bus.

Ricky hated these extra-long busses they made by sticking two buses together and linking the middle with an accordion-looking thing. That thing was made out of some kind of flexible plastic that groaned and creaked when the bus went over potholes, and its floor was a stiff circle that rotated when the bus turned. It was dark as fuck in that part of the bus, and within that dark, creaky, moving fuckbox were two pairs of seats. Ricky had always assumed that if the bus were to make a sharp turn and fishtail, the two halves would spin out and break apart, and the niggas sitting in the accordion seats would take all the punishment. Their skulls would be crushed, arms yanked off the torso, and whatever bits remained would shoot straight into the pavement. Ricky wanted to see if Houellebecq would be scared. "You sit in the fuckbox," Ricky said. He directed Houellebecq to the fuckbox seats.

"I want to look out the window," Houellebecq said.

"You can see the window if you stretch your neck," Ricky said.

Houellebecq hovered over the fuckbox seat, and then darted toward one of the many empty seats on the bus. Just as Houellebecq's ass was about to hit the seat, Ricky gave him a hearty shove. Houellebecq tumbled into the circle. "Ha ha. They call you Mister Middle Bus . . . My nigga . . . ," Ricky said.

Houellebecq crawled to one of the fuckbox seats and hoisted himself half onto it. He sat there looking like he was deep in thought. "And I bet they call you Mister Macho Man," he said.

"I called your moms Macho Man last night, nigga," Ricky said.

"My mother is dead," Houellebecq said.

•

The city grew ever more dirty and abandoned as the bus traveled west. The coffee shops, art galleries, and high-rise condo buildings were replaced by taco shops and auto repair centers, which were in turn replaced by abandoned warehouses, scrap yards, and squat, run-down houses. The bus changed as well. When Houellebecq and Ricky had boarded, some ten or fifteen well-dressed whites got on with them. Block by block, these whites exited the bus, replaced at first by small groups of whites, Latinos, and blacks, but later by lone black men or mothers with two or three kids. The bus's racial makeup went from nearly entirely white to nearly entirely black.

"There a bridge coming up, homie," Ricky said.

"Oh?" Houellebecq said.

"As soon as we go under that bridge, you won't see a single white person on this bus. Unless someone sticks a mirror in your face."

"The white people know not to go past these elevated tracks?"

"Naw, nigga, it ain't like that. They just ain't cross it. They got no reason to, they got their own shit back there. They ain't even know any of this shit exists," Ricky said.

Houellebecq stretched his neck to look out the window. He saw a factory with every window boarded up and an empty, overgrown lot. "But what is out here?"

"Well," Ricky said, "we got a Dunkin Donut. Not even a Starbucks. You go south, north, or west, and there ain't even a Dunkin Donut. We got one Dunkin Donut that serves six miles of the hood. And it's the worst one in the city. It's the only Dunkin that give you rotten old watered down coffee."

"So the ghetto in Chicago consists of this part of town?"

Ricky leaned back in his seat and thought about that. "Naw nigga . . . The ghetto, the ghetto goes on forever. Shit, let me think about it . . . So this shit is technically West Humboldt Park. Then you got Austin to the west. South of here you got Garfield Park and Lawndale, then you got Douglas Park. All of that shit is fucked up. Only thing that's easy to get there is heroin. And that's just the West Side. Then you got the South Side: Englewood, Auburn Gresham . . . To be honest, I don't know shit about down South, just that it's bigger than the West Side. I mean, you could start walking south from right here and you'd basically never get out. You'd never see shit but niggas slinging drugs, old people sitting out on the porch, and bombed out buildings."

"So these parts of the city are unknown to whites," Houellebecq said.

"Yea nigga. Except to the junkies . . . If you white on the West Side, you buying dope."

They got off the bus at a street lined with nearly identical buildings, hundred-year-old two-flats. Their original bricks had fallen out long ago. Ricky looked with affection at the shitty siding that he'd watched melt on hot summer days and the homemade wood porches on which he'd spent many a summer night. There was trash on the sidewalk and in the gutters, but the lawns were decently maintained. "This does not look so bad," Houellebecq said.

"That's cause this street is Puerto Rican, not black. Bet you anything all this trash came from the blacks."

"Where are we going?" Houellebecq said.

"Home, nigga."

"But I need to smoke."

"Yeah we gonna smoke."

"Give me a cigarette now."

"I don't smoke."

"You just said you smoked."

Ricky turned around and smiled, showing a rotten tooth. "I don't smoke, nigga. I smoke. Know what I'm saying?"

"I do not know what you are saying, nor do I care about your personal practices. I would just like a cigarette."

"Damn nigga, fine. We'll hit up the corner store."

They walked until they reached the end of the block. The building at the corner had a row of windows pasted over with yellow signs advertising meat, onions, alcohol, and cigarettes. On the sidewalk lay what appeared to be loose chunks of hair. "Ratchet ass neighborhood hos must have been wilding out last night," Ricky said.

"Is this real human hair?" Houellebecq said.

"Fuck! This a weave, nigga. Damn, why I gotta explain everything to you."

"Does this weave occur elsewhere? There are people in the ghetto leaving the weave on the sidewalk?"

"Oh my god nigga. Ain't no one leave it unless it get torn off they head. That shit's expensive."

Ricky pushed open the door, which dinged a little bell. A little old Puerto Rican man leaned over the counter to look at them. A thick wall of plastic separated the man, along with the cash register and a wall of cigarettes and hard alcohol, from the rest of the store. Houellebecq stepped up to the plastic and studied the cigarettes, but there was no way to make sense of the rows of boxes and prices. There were brands he recognized from popular culture, but he had never smoked any of the cigarettes that were on offer. "Shopkeeper, I would like you to tell me what is your best cigarette."

The shopkeeper looked at Houellebecq with suspicion. "I don't smoke. You buy."

Houellebecq was beginning to get upset that even here, in the "American Ghetto," his type was reviled and spat on. Was there nowhere that a smoker could garner the proper respect? Smoking was but a simple lifestyle choice, a low-to-moderate vice that at worst cut a few years from the gruesome and boring epilogue of life, and he was sick and tired of seeing the faces people made when presented with a smoker. "Do you have a problem with smoking, even though it makes you a magnificent profit?"

The shopkeeper pointed at a handwritten sign that said "Cook County Taxes on a Box of Cigarettes: $7.05."

Ricky bumped into Houellebecq and shoved him aside. "Don't bug the man." He acknowledged the shopkeeper and said, "Let me get two packs of Newports. Shorts."

The shopkeeper took the green boxes from the shelf and set them on the counter. He looked relieved. Ricky looked at Houellebecq, indicating that he needed to pay now. Houellebecq tilted his head back. "I do not even know if I like these."

"Nigga, if you live around here you smoke Newports. Any of these other cigarettes," he said, gesturing at the wall of boxes, "has been here since the store opened. Now pay the man."

Houellebecq handed over Edward Michaels' credit card. The shopkeeper ran it through the machine and waited. He ran it through again, and again, and then threw the card back at Ricky. Ricky looked at the card. "Edward Michaels? You steal this shit, nigga?"

Houellebecq was flabbergasted. Ricky groaned. "Why the fuck you tryna pass off bad credit cards in here?" Ricky threw a couple crumpled bills on the counter. He grabbed the packs of smokes, and then grabbed Houellebecq by the collar and dragged him out of the store. "Next time I go in there that old ass nigga is gonna call the cops on me. Fuck, man. Now I gotta walk three extra blocks every time I need to hit up the corner store."

"The card was not stolen. It was given to me for my new identity. I thought there would be more than a $500 limit on it. This is ludicrous," Houellebecq said.

"New identity, nigga?"

"Yes, Jack Reacher provided me with a new identity while I was to hide from my assassin in the United States."

"Hahaha," Ricky said and stormed down the street. Houellebecq frantically followed him. "So you dead as fuck in Europe, and here you're an all new somebody else. Nigga they stole your money. You're fucked nigga. You ain't got me for shit either, you ain't even exist nigga. You fucked, nigga, you fucked."

"I am confident that I can reclaim my identity," Houellebecq said breathlessly.

"You ass up, nigga. That ain't the place to be confident of anything," Ricky said.

Houellebecq thought he would have to call Beigbeder, definitely Beigbeder. Beigbeder could be trusted, and more importantly, Beigbeder had a level of societal respect and intimacy with Houellebecq that would allow him to realistically communicate with the press.

Houellebecq took a pack of cigarettes from Ricky and shook one out. While they walked, he smoked and thought. This "Newport" was quite strong and pleasant—he could see why everybody in the American ghetto smoked it . . . But what did other Americans smoke?

They approached the side door of one of the similar two-story brick houses on the block. "Mi basement es su basement," Ricky said. "You only owe me $200 a month rent. Hahah. I wasn't gonna charge you til I found out that you a broke ass nobody."

"You can be sure I will only be here a few days, long enough to sort things out,"

Houellebecq said.

"What happened to the new stage of your life, nigga?"

"I am too old to enter any new stages. I just want to live with my money in a house on the coast."

"You ain't got any money. Believe," Ricky said. "You gonna write my book in a basement on the West Side." Ricky opened the door and barged in.

Houellebecq looked around. He had never been in a room with such a low ceiling. He saw that the walls were black with some sort of plant growth and noticed that the air was sour. He felt like he was being choked. Only rats could live in a place like this.

Ricky plopped on the couch and inspected a pile of broken glass on the coffee table. "Damn, forgot I busted up my bong." He opened a drawer in the coffee table and took out a dusty, burnt bowl and a small wooden box. He removed a lump of marijuana from the box and began breaking it into tiny pieces which he fit carefully into the bowl. He lit it and inhaled deeply. While Ricky held in the smoke his face looked like a constipated Buddha. "Fuuuuuuuck," he exhaled. The smell was pungent. "Sit your ass down and smoke with me," Ricky said.

Houellebecq had no interest in this juvenile pastime. "I respectfully 'just say no.'"

"More for me," Ricky said. "You got shit to do, nigga? This is life." He took another hit from the bowl. "Come on. I can't stand smoking by myself with another nigga around."

This sudden, warped confession of a desire for companionship surprised Houellebecq. He had often observed that there were many people in life not worth talking to—a single word was a profound waste of mental exertion—but Ricky possessed a special brand of charm, stupidity, and pathos that somehow exempted him from this general principle. Houellebecq had noticed it particularly in the manner in which Ricky had caught those chocolates with his mouth.

Houellebecq sat down next to Ricky and took the bowl. "I must warn you that marijuana is wasted on me," Houellebecq said. "I receive no joy or pleasure but rather paranoia and fear."

"Fuck you talkin about? Why you got a big idea about every little old thing?"

"I am hopelessly forthright," Houellebecq said.

"Fuck . . . Just hit the bowl, nigga."

Houellebecq shyly took a hit. The smoke pounded his lungs like ten thousand Eastern European cigarettes of the lowest quality. He coughed and hacked, expelling the marijuana in fits and gasps.

"Puff puff pass nigga," Ricky said, cackling and rolling around on the couch.

Houellebecq took another hit. This time he made a better effort, holding the smoke in for a few seconds. Immediately he could feel precisely how soft his teeth were . . . He went to work tonguing his teeth, hoping that Ricky wasn't watching. Houellebecq consoled himself by thinking that everyone had bodily tics and nobody ever noticed them.

"Pass it back, nigga," Ricky said. He took the bowl and smoked. After his hit, he looked at Houellebecq, laughed, and said, "You funny as hell, bro." He took another hit and passed the bowl back to Houellebecq.

A spike of shame shot through Houellebecq. Ricky had noticed after all! "Please, no more," Houellebecq said and immediately stopped tonguing his teeth.

"Come on, it's good shit," Ricky said. "If you smoke with me, you gonna get blazed."

"Please, go ahead without me," Houellebecq said. He spoke too fast, he thought, he should have gone slower, more carefully, because the words were wrong, they sounded too significant, too heavy, they didn't correctly express what he meant, and he instantly wanted to clarify what he meant, but at the same time was terrified of speaking more, speaking slowly like a retard, or too fast with the wrong inflections, and having Ricky listen to him. "Listen to him judge," Houellebecq said.

Houellebecq grabbed a nearby blanket and draped it over his face. He was overcome by the multiplicity of its moist smells, but the darkness it provided filled him with relief. He could hear Ricky laughing from outside the blanket. Houellebecq pulled it back ever so slightly so he could peek at the frightening, amiable baboon. Ricky too had somehow turned against him, he thought, then dimly realized that Ricky was *against him from the beginning*. Why did Houellebecq agree to smoke this horrible drug? He would give anything to undo it. He stared glumly at the coffee table, where he saw the pale blue American edition of *The Elementary Particles*. "My book! You have been gathering information to use against me."

"You weren't kidding about getting paranoid, nigga," Ricky said. "Now that you paying my rent, we sorta bros, and I'll tell you about how your book got there. This shit kinda all your fault," Ricky said. He jumped to his feet and fixed his attention on the wall behind Houellebecq's head. "Is that a fuck spider dangling?"

It took all of Houellebecq's self-control not to look or react. Ricky climbed onto the couch and swatted the wall with his big meat-hand. "Smeared!"

"I will not pay your rent," Houellebecq said slowly.

"Get back under the stank blanket, little old man nigga," Ricky said. He burst into giggles and sank into his place on the couch. "That blanket a bath towel. Hehe."

Houellebecq obediently draped the blanket over his eyes, then instantly regretted obeying Ricky and threw the blanket off. "Peek-a-boo playing ass nigga!" Ricky howled. Houellebecq put the blanket back over his eyes, for good. Ricky began to talk.

"Man, you funny as fuck. Did I say that shit already? Hiding your old ass under that towel like that. Shit. What was I tryna say before? Oh, shit. See, I had this little fine thing coming around to kick it with my old fucked up ass. She had them big bright eyes. Skin so smooth that a freckle was like a . . . fuck, fuck if I know, like a single bean on a plate of rice? Nah, *arroz con leche*, hombre. Smooooth. We went way back. I knew her older sis, and shorty looked up to me like whoa. Hold up, let me tell it like how it was. My life story. Hehe.

"The streets kind of raised me. I was always in the streets since I was young. I would always play like I was a good child. But for hours when I was supposed to be in bed, I watched and listened to the gangsters on the block where we lived. I was fascinated by their lifestyle, and fuck if I ain't want to be like them.

"Yo, tell me if I need to shut up. Niggas always telling me I run my mouth whenever I smoke."

From under the towel, Houellebecq mumbled, "Please go on. I have no desire to speak." Houellebecq was feeling better now that he had no apparent cause to move, speak, or otherwise attempt to interact normally.

"I got to a point in my life where I wanted to be a drug dealer. It was hard work but I liked how fast you reaped the benefits. When I first started hustling on the streets in Chicago, the money I made was cool, but as I got a little older, I realized that it just wasn't fast enough. Too much competition. I decided to take my show on the road. Long story short, I got to running the dope game out in the burbs.

"My bad, dog, I been talking shit for a minute now. But I was getting around to Elvia—my girl's name is Elvia. Shit in the burbs fell apart hard. All my boys was dead and I was done. I barely escaped still breathing. Around then, Elvia's sister skipped town with some crackhead. Not that I'd been running steady with her. At some point she was sort of *cual quiera*. I'd seen her with a couple of my boys. I think them disappearing freaked her out, you know.

"Aite. So Elvia's sis skipped out. Her parents were pretty broke up. It felt like the right thing to do to go over there and chill with them, seeing as I was the one that fucked everything up, and knowing how my moms felt when my little bro ran off. So I checked up on them, hell, I smoked them out sometimes. Elvia started to want to hang and smoke. So I got to know her a bit. Man, she was young though, and shit kinda creeped me out, but shit, plenty of girls younger than her working the street.

"Shit, all this soft as hell. I was getting around to saying that Elvia kinda bunked up with me. Like she was my girl girl, you know. At some point, she starts going on about your book, nigga. Saying I'm some sort of aging nigga with a deathwish, saying I'm only with her cause she young and shit, just like the niggas in your book. I couldn't understand where she was getting this shit from. Or why she gave a fuck what some French nigga like you wrote about old white men jerking ill all the way in

Europe. Turns out some college boy was filling her head with ideas.

"Them ideas was turning Elvia bad. She forgot about her family, told me she hated cleaning up after them, how she was gonna leave them behind and hated that they didn't let her go to college out of state. Fuck is that shit? Ain't no one around here needs school and ain't no one got money to pay for college anyway, she was lucky to get enrolled for Harold Washington. Her parents was calling me up asking me what was going on with her, why she was getting so mean, and asking me when we was gonna *casarnos*, get married, you know, but she wasn't having that shit. Said that me and her wasn't sexually compatible, that she was an Esther from one of your books, a girl who should have been out enjoying her youth with other young people, that she coulda been getting nice shit from rich guys, and she was wasting her time fucking around with a fucked up old nigga like me who was just gonna get older and more fucked up.

"That's when I read your book. I saw you, some random ass French nigga, getting mass power and pussy from scribbling some boring old ideas. There's a word for that shit—manipulation. And that college boy was doing the same thing to Elvia, except it was easier for him cause he ain't even need to write shit down himself. He just point at your ass and get the pussy that way. And it's the weak who lap that shit up, it ain't no different from the drug game. I don't know if Elvia was weak-minded, maybe she was just young. Anyway I loved her."

Houellebecq was shocked. He pulled the corner of the towel until it came off his face and he could see the man sitting beside him. "So you came after me," Houellebecq said. "I think you are right about me, but what you say is true of all writers. Do I deserve to die for it? That is a curious thought, one I have often had myself." Houellebecq paused. Ricky said nothing. "The tragedy of your story is that Elvia misunderstood my work. I critique, I do not exalt the Western World."

"It doesn't matter what you wanted, nigga. What matters is what Elvia got out of it. That's what's real." Ricky scowled at Houellebecq, then turned away and snatched the bowl. He held the lighter to the blackened weed. "Damn, this is cashed. So here's what's up." He set the bowl down and turned back to Houellebecq. "Like I been saying, we writing together now. I'ma make sure your famous words is gonna come out right."

Houellebecq almost wanted to laugh while he felt a scream of rage course through his body. "Do you not realize that all you just said applies to you as a writer as well? If you write about smoking marijuana, some woman in Guatemala might murder her infant child and say it was your idea. People are free to interpret your work however they please. Only the basest idiots . . ." Houellebecq cut himself off. He didn't want to insult Ricky or Elvia, despite their profligate stupidity.

"One base idiot with another, we gonna write a book!" Ricky shouted. He stomped to the other room. Houellebecq could see him digging around in the blankets of a mattress on the floor. Ricky pulled out a small laptop and charged at Houellebecq with it. "Page one," Ricky said, plopping down on the couch and ripping open the screen. "Chapter name, 'A Poor Mexican Grows Up Among His Kind.' Subchapter name, 'Stealin and Dealin in the Hood.'"

Houellebecq quickly stood up and moved away from the couch. He covered his shoulders with the towel and began to shout at Ricky. "I have told you that I write in private, in the utmost secrecy, I do not collaborate in literature, I do not collaborate in anything, I will not be your collaborator, I will not stay here with you and pretend to be dead! You agreed to help me gather material for a novel! A novel, let me remind you, that already has a plot!" Houellebecq felt queasy, angry, and ludicrous, stoned and clinging to a dirty towel. This drama had lost all interest, and he wished he had run for help in the New York airport. "I barely care to write at all. I would like to go to sleep."

Ricky closed the computer. "Aite, you can sleep on it. You need to hard think about your position. Ass up, nigga," Ricky said. "You take the bedroom. Ain't no windows in there. I'ma bed down on the couch next to the door. Guard duty, nigga."

•

Houellebecq sat on the mattress. The springs gave way; he could feel the floor. He lay in the dark and closed his eyes. He was still feeling the effects of the marijuana. His thoughts were greasy and slow, but the impetus to reclaim his identity persisted. It turned out that the inert nothingness of his life on the coast had been beautiful and wildly desirable. Even acknowledging the likely fallaciousness of such a thought—all things seemed rosy in retrospect— Houellebecq knew that he must return.

Houellebecq heard Ricky snoring in the other room. Houellebecq inched Jack Reacher's phone from his pocket. He stared at the luminescent yellow numbers on the keypad and dialed Beigbeder's number. It would be early morning in Paris, and Beigbeder was surely lying in bed in a state of agonized half-awareness at the conclusion of a night of insomnia. He would appreciate this unexpected stimulus. Perhaps he'd even fly to Chicago and fuck Ricky's "Elvia."

The phone rang endlessly. Just when Houellebecq began to doubt he had dialed correctly, a woman answered.

Houellebecq recognized the voice of Apollinariya, Beigbeder's beautiful young Russian girl. "*Puis-je parler à Frédéric?*" Houellebecq asked.

Houellebecq heard her inhale sharply. "*Vous ne saviez pas? Il est mort. Assassiné.*"

"*Quand?*"

"Il y a deux semaines." She began to sob.

"Je ne sais pas. Je vous prie de bien vouloir accepter mes sincères condoléances," Houellebecq said and hung up. So they killed Beigbeder too. His agent's death had meant nothing: agents are utterly replaceable. His mother's death was inconsequential, even expected. In his novels he had already followed the Freudian implications of her mothering to their logical conclusions. Beigbeder was different. He was one of Houellebecq's contemporaries. For the first time Houellebecq felt the circle around him to be closing. There would be no more parties worth attending.

No matter, Houellebecq thought. There was still a way out of this. All he had to do was inform the world that he was still alive. Simple, in a sense, but Houellebecq had no clear idea how to go about it. He considered calling the authorities, but he had no proof that he was Michel Houellebecq and not Edward Michaels. He could reveal himself on the Internet, perhaps claim that his apparent death was a publicity stunt. Or another Internet hoax. He could draft a press release, but he had no agent to disseminate it. Perhaps he could register a Twitter? Write to American journalists who were familiar with his work?

Houellebecq was unsatisfied with those ideas. Nevertheless, he turned on the phone and scrolled through its tiny menus in search of a browser. He located the language preferences, address book, alarm and calculator functionalities, and several card games. It was difficult for Houellebecq to believe that any modern phone could not connect to the Internet. Hoping to find a secret menu, he mashed buttons in random combinations. Finally, gleefully, he saw something suggesting the phone had a connection to the Internet. The options included sports scores, news, stocks, trends, and brand names. He clicked news and waited for minutes as it loaded. The page had nothing but a list of news stories. There was no URL and no ostensible way to navigate back or elsewhere on the web. He was trapped on this page. There was no choice but to click on one of the headlines. "Saturated fat DOESN'T cause heart disease after all."

Houellebecq fell asleep waiting for the page to load.

Michel Houellebecq's style is praised as a blending of
Gustave Flaubert, Honoré de Balzac, and Albert Camus.
—The European Graduate School

Ricky awoke in terror and reached for the knife he kept under his mattress. There was no knife; he was on the couch. He sighed and lay back down. The *patos* had been after him in his dreams again. "Fucking faggots!"

Ricky went to take a piss. He was in a bad mood. It was Houellebecq's fault for making Ricky sleep on the couch. That bobo gonna pay for this, Ricky thought. He sure as fuck gonna write today. He flushed the toilet and watched the pissy water flood up from the shower drain.

Ricky pushed open the bedroom door. Houellebecq had not bothered untangling the wads of blankets at the foot of the bed, and his body sprawled across the mattress looked like a smashed spider. His head was thrown back and a line of spit was running from his mouth. Ricky could see the damp spot where it had pooled. "Ready to write, nigga?"

Houellebecq didn't move or open his eyes. "Wake up, dog. I called up one of my boys from back in the day. He a prince now with the Maniac Latin Disciples. The nigga done ordered the deaths of like . . . Fifty niggas."

Houellebecq opened his eyes. "Maniac?"

"Yeah, Maniac. Name come from back when a Latin Disciple was facing time for dealing dope. The judge starts reading the sentence, and the Disciple screams "maniac." So the judge adds a year for interrupting the sentence, and the nigga screams "maniac" again. Old judge gives him some more years and he screams again. Shit goes back and forth like that until, legend has it, the cops get fed up and throw him out the court window. Hehe. Shit's probably fake."

Houellebecq sat up. "You say you know this man who screamed 'maniac?'"

"Pete the Burner? Fuck no. Like I said, ain't no one know if he exist or not. Just some shit the niggas like to talk about when they high to think they hard. I know Gotchu D Amor."

"Gotchu D Amor . . . That is wonderful." Houellebecq pulled out a Newport and lit up, taking one of the longest drags Ricky had ever seen. "What sort of information can this Gotchu provide?"

"Gotchu? Shit, Gotchu know it all. Come on, get your ass ready and let's hit it."

Houellebecq stood up. "I am ready," he said. They shambled out of the basement, Houellebecq still smoking. A cold wind was blowing. An empty bag of cookies had made its way to the cement in front of Ricky's door. Ricky kicked it out of the way. They made their way down the block and waited for the bus that went east.

On the bus, Houellebecq seemed suspicious. "We are going back the way we came? I thought the ghetto continued farther west and south."

"Oh," Ricky said. "You know, Gotchu done moved up in the world. Hehe. Anyway, we only going a few blocks."

They exited the bus in front of a car parts store. Ricky crossed the street and Houellebecq followed. They were going into a tinted glass door with flyers pasted over it.

Ricky had seen this café all the time but had never gone in. He immediately wanted to leave. There was a long, old-fashioned wood bar against one wall. Bearded white boys wearing little hats were smiling and fiddling with stainless steel coffee machines behind the counter. On the other wall, at several cafe tables, girls with blue hair and short skirts were looking at Facebook and cradling big mugs of coffee. Some kind of fucked up dubstep with a whining British singer was blaring so loud that Ricky's head started spinning. People write in here? Ricky thought. Maybe he'd been wrong.

"Why are we here?" Houellebecq asked. "This is some kind of cafe for juveniles playing at artists."

"Calm down, nigga. Gotchu told us to meet him here. I ain't like this place either."

They walked to the counter. When the bearded nigga approached them and smiled, Ricky found himself speechless. Houellebecq ordered two coffees. Ricky paid.

The coffees came in the gigantic mugs like the girls'. Ricky dumped half of his in the trash and filled it back to the top with cream and sugar. Houellebecq gave Ricky a dirty look and made a show of sipping the black coffee. "That shit rot your guts, man," Ricky said.

They sat at a table near the back. Ricky took his laptop out of his backpack. He pushed it to Houellebecq with the word processor open. "What are you doing?" Houellebecq said. "Where is Gotchu?"

"Gotchu's coming. We might as well get some writing done while we in the place where it get done. Am I right?" Ricky said.

"I have never written in a place like this. Only *poseurs* write in places like this. I require privacy and silence, neither of which are currently present."

Ricky looked at the people in the cafe. They were all playing on laptops. "Man, nigga, can't you just like, take some notes or something?"

Houellebecq glared at Ricky. In the silence they both looked at the people at the table next to them. A woman with a nose piercing was saying that she hasn't done any performance art since last summer. The two men with her were nodding solemnly. One of them had dreadlocks and was carrying a staff with ornaments and strings tied to the end. A stranger from the next table leaned over and said that he knew of a new performance space in the city. Everyone at the table looked at him with interest.

"I must leave this place," Houellebecq said.

"I feel you, but we came all the way here."

"It was only a few blocks. We can walk."

They both stared grimly at their coffee. "I take it that Gotchu is not coming?" Houellebecq said.

"Got you . . . Haha," Ricky said. Houellebecq's face crumpled in a helpless, furious pout. "Please take some notes, dog. Do I gotta do something to convince you?"

"I will write a sketch of my novel to satisfy you. I will only briefly indicate what has long been my plan, then we will leave. I refuse to create in your presence."

"Can I get you a cookie or something?"

Houellebecq seemed to think about it. "Yes. A croissant."

The delay of Ricky fetching the croissant eased some of the tension. Houellebecq tore off long strips of croissant and tapped on Ricky's computer. Ricky obediently looked away. He noticed with horror that many people in the cafe were Mexican and Puerto Rican. They were wearing cutesy fedoras and old-timey suspenders the same way the whiteboys did, looking even more smug and happy to be in there. Ricky looked down at his baggy sweatpants, old Reeboks, and gummy Fila hoodie. Fuck, he thought, I guess I ain't on point. But neither is those niggas . . . Were they even real Mexicans?

"I am done," Houellebecq announced. Ricky pulled his chair to the other side of the table to take a look.

A GENIUS URBAN PLANNER AT THE END OF HIS LIFE INVENTS PLAN THAT CHANGES SOCIAL LANDSCAPE FOR ALL TIME (as a child, he loves animals) (success in field but little success in love [women troubles])

familial, intellectual, sociological genealogy—many insights. genealogy of the city genesis of idea - failure of Le Corbusier, impending failure of post-modern planning ideas, new cities, must planned cities fail? Lucio Costa etc.

Extremely sexy Latina, 17-year-old, reads Houellebecq.

Ricky turned red when he read the last line. "What the fuck you mean extremely sexy Latina reads Houellebecq, nigga?" Ricky demanded.

"Her name is Gotcha . . . Gotcha Fucking Imbecile." Houellebecq cackled briefly before coughing his ass off. "I need to smoke," he said.

They went out front and Houellebecq lit a cigarette. Nearby a black guy in khaki pants and a white guy with a leather jacket were discussing McDonald's. "It's hard to buy the healthy food there. The salad has a lot of calories, and it's more expensive," the white guy said.

"Yeah, I quit eating McDonald's for a year after I saw *Super Size Me*. Now they came out with that movie where the guy lost weight," the black guy said. "So I'm like, fuck it, what can you really know?"

"HAHAHA!" the white guy said. "But we gotta take care of our bodies man."

"No doubt, yeah, no doubt," the black guy said.

Fuck these niggas, Ricky thought. He looked at Houellebecq and knew that Houellebecq was thinking the same thing. It was the first time he felt something like a friendly feeling for Houellebecq. "So what's up nigga," Ricky said, "you still wanna bounce? I can introduce you to some homies tomorrow, for real this time."

"It is unnecessary. I will be booking a flight tonight," Houellebecq said. "If you would permit me to stay with you for a few days until I fly out."

"Aite, nigga, that's cool. You got the money?"

Houellebecq scowled. "It will be a cheap seat. Coach," he said.

"You know, if you need to make some cash, you still got the chance to learn the ins and outs of the hood. I still know some niggas who'll let you cop, maybe they even give you a corner for a day. Hehe."

They walked west. Houellebecq lit another cigarette. Ricky looked around, hoping there weren't any bangers out who might see him with this lame . . . "You know," he said, "this right here used to belong to Latin Kings. That was before somebody got capped and Damen 26 took over for a minute. Niggas would kill each other over these corners. Niggas held their heads up high. People used to be scared of the gangs. Now there's so many white folk around that the bangers is embarrassed to be out unless they cruising at 3 a.m."

"In France, the poor have been exiled to the most remote regions of the country. They call themselves *Les Invisibles*," Houellebecq said. "Nobody sees them. Nobody sees how they live."

"It be the same here if them whites keep moving west."

"Mixed income neighborhoods are an impossible dream the politicians use to seduce social liberals."

"Huh . . . Well, this my block." Ricky took a sharp turn at the intersection and paused, gazing toward the next intersection. "You talking mixed income? See those identical houses down there, the ones that don't look like these old ones? Thems is no income. Those motherfuckers are CHA, Chicago Housing Authority. Section eight. Some private company busted in here in the 90s, got the lots for a dollar cause they had the crooked alderman in they pockets, tore down a bunch of old buildings, built those things, and sold them to the city for billions of dollars. As for the niggas inside, well, you ain't got a job, you pop out a few kids, and then you can put yourself on the city's public housing roster. Wait a few years and you get a free ride in one of those bitches. The Ricans and Mexicans around here were pissed cause their family worked hard to buy the old slums. They paid with blood, sweat, and tears. Meanwhile, those new CHA houses is the nicest places on the block. Worst part is suddenly the neighborhood's black and dirty. Wasn't no blacks here before." Ricky took off jogging back home. Houellebecq clumsily chased him.

By the time Houellebecq walked in the door, Ricky was getting ready to take a hit. "You want some more weed, nigga?" Ricky laughed.

"I will go to sleep," Houellebecq said.

"So what's up," Ricky said. "You gonna write that whole book while you asleep?"

"I do not plan to write."

Ricky rolled his eyes and laughed like a hyena, shooting smoke out his nostrils. "Not this again. What's your problem? You need me to leave you alone? Or is these surroundings not classy enough for an author?" Ricky said, making a sweeping gesture that included the mold on the walls and the glass-block windows.

"The squalor has a certain charm. But our situation, as I have said, does not provide the level of privacy and stability that is required for one to write an entire book," Houellebecq said. "I would not be able to concentrate."

"Oh, is that right," Ricky said. "Look, nigga, you can take my computer in the room and wild out. I'll leave your ass alone. It can be as private as you want. I just want to help you. Anyway, I'll just write my own book while you write yours. I got pen and paper and this couch."

"Perhaps I will take your computer. But I will not guarantee anything," Houellebecq said.

Nigga thirsty to get that computer, Ricky thought. If he didn't know that Houellebecq was broke, he'd think the nigga was actually gonna book a flight. "Aite, here you go," Ricky said, offering the tiny laptop to Houellebecq.

"Thank you," Houellebecq said, taking the laptop and scuttling to Ricky's bedroom. As soon as the door closed, Ricky went to the kitchen. He poured a generous helping of vodka into two glasses. Rummaging in the fridge, he found a carton of orange juice. Damn, this shit been in here for longer than I can remember, he thought. Maybe he had some tonic water.

He opened a kitchen drawer and took out a pill bottle with the label ripped off. Anybody gonna concentrate with this, Ricky thought, chuckling to himself. He used the bottom of the vodka bottle to crush two pills and poured the powder in equal parts into each glass. He topped the vodka-and-pill mixture with tap water and saw with horror that the powder floated on top. The taste wouldn't be disguised. He filled the glasses to the top with a Modelo beer and mixed it hard. "Hey," he shouted, banging on the door. "Before you balls deep in literature, want a drink?"

"Thank you," Houellebecq said, opening the door just enough to reach out his hand. Ricky heard Houellebecq take a sip and gag. "What is this?"

"An American cocktail *especial*," Ricky said. "It's alcohol ain't it?" Ricky drained his glass in one gulp. "It's aite if you pound it."

Ricky found a pen on the floor and went to get paper from his old school stuff. Ricky's mom had moved all his kid things to the basement when Ricky had officially moved back home, as if he'd wanted them. The dusty cardboard boxes were still stacked in a corner.

He opened one of the boxes. On the top was a piece of construction paper with a unicorn Ricky had drawn in the first grade . . . Something made Ricky tear the paper up. He wanted to dump all this school shit outside . . . Ricky licked his lips and took out an old notebook he'd had in high school. It reminded him of how he failed algebra twice. Well, this notebook gonna be a book now, he thought.

Ricky returned to the couch. He tore out the old pieces of paper that had math equations on them, but left the pages where he had doodled gang signs. Disciples, he thought. He still liked the way the old English Ds looked. "My Novel," he wrote largely. What was it he'd said to Houellebecq last night? "Dope and the Dopey Dopes Pushing It?" "Real Niggas Rep the Hood?" "A Little Boy with a Big Dream (Mexican)?" Fuck, Ricky thought. Writing is hard. Why did he wanna do this shit again? He could never compete with a white European hotshot like Houellebecq. Hate to admit it, Ricky thought, but that nigga's smart as fuck.

Ricky decided to write about Elvia. He could work it into the later part of the book once he wrote the "genealogy." Tomorrow, probably.

> I loved her. She could have been the queen of my heart but I had to put her down. Boom. I wish that was the way it'd gone down. She left me. Every part of her. Her jugs, her legs, her puss, went away. Or was it me who went away to Spain?

Ricky's heart was pounding, not from laying out the bare bones of his romance, but rather from the speed he'd poured into the cocktail. He stared at the words on the paper. This shit is fucked up, he thought. What were you even supposed to write? He wondered how Houellebecq was doing.

Ricky, notepad in hand, crept over to the bedroom door. He scrawled out, "Bro, didn't want to disturb you, so wrote this note. How you doing bro? I can't concentrate. Bout to give up, you were write. Signed, me." He spent a couple minutes drawing an elaborate old English D before slipping the paper under the door.

He pressed his ear to the door, but didn't hear anything. Houellebecq must not have seen the note. "Psst," Ricky said. He heard some movement and the paper rustle.

Houellebecq yanked the door open. Nigga was wild eyed and crazy looking. Must have been a writing tornado come through. "Why is it I am unable to sleep?"

"Cause you're suppose to be writing."

Houellebecq pushed past Ricky and sat on the couch. He poured a few nuggets of weed out from their baggy and started breaking them up, piling them on the coffee table. "You tryna smoke?" Ricky said.

"No, I am facilitating the process of their dissolution, so that you do not have to do it later," Houellebecq said.

"Fuck, nigga, they gonna get stale. Knock that off." Ricky sat down next to Houellebecq and eyed the nuggets of weed. The little bits and pieces were driving him crazy. He swept them into his hand and started rolling them together. "You don't fuck with a man's stash," he said, continuing to roll the weed into a little ball.

Houellebecq kept breaking the weed up. Ricky kept rolling it back together.

"What is that black material on the walls?"

"Oh, that? That mold, nigga. Some sorta water getting into the walls. Then the shit just grow," Ricky said. "Now the little brownish spots, if that's what you talking about, those is bug-smears. Mainly spider-smears. I hate them danglers."

Houellebecq stopped breaking up the weed and dropped it all on the coffee table. "The spiders are attracted by the mold, and the mold is probably getting in the marijuana."

"First off, don't mention spiders in my house. Second, hell no the mold ain't getting in the weed, homie, the weed is getting in the mold."

"What?"

"Weed stops mold from growing. Weed green, mold black, every nigga know those colors against each other."

"White is the opposite of black, and black contains all the colors, although white light too contains all of the colors."

"This place dark as fuck. No light get in here, sunup or sundown. And what you saying, white light contains all the colors? Like light some kind of master white? You a racist on top of being old and French?"

"Your characterization of old French men is uncannily accurate, although it does not apply to me."

"Oh, so you some kind of special old white racist?"

"We are simply talking about the mold," Houellebecq said.

"Oh, the mold?" Ricky shouted and stood up. He ran to the wall at the front of the house, where the mold grew thickest, and kicked with all his might. The drywall caved in. He turned around and started donkey kicking it. Hunks of moldy drywall shot across the floor and fell between the studs with a hollow clatter.

Houellebecq got up and knelt in front of the hole. He inspected the torn drywall, touching it gingerly, putting his nose up to it, sniffing, and then examining his finger. "The entire wall is suffused with this organism," he said.

"Fuck!" Ricky shouted. "Shit's all up everywhere!" He ran to the cardboard box where his mom had put his criming tools from his teen years. He took out a hammer and slid it across the floor to Houellebecq. "Come on, nigga, help me out here," Ricky said, pulling out a small crowbar that once pried open windows.

Houellebecq grabbed the hammer and put the claw in the edge of the hole. He feebly pulled the hammer and tore a few inches out of the wall. Ricky laughed.

"Let me show you how to fuck some shit up," Ricky said. He walked to the basement's entrance and pointed at the mold growing on either side of the door. "See that shit?" Ricky lifted the crowbar over his head and punched it straight through the drywall. Then he brought his full weight down on the crowbar, ripping a gash that went nearly from the ceiling to the floor. "You gotta hit it like it fucked your mama!"

Houellebecq slammed the hammer into the wall a few times, making several golfball-sized holes. "Hit it some more!" Ricky crooned. Houellebecq hit the same portion of the wall until gigantic chunks started falling and cracking on the floor. The entire basement was filling with dust. Ricky went to the other side of the door and bashed the wall at random with the crowbar.

"Heyyyy, Rickyyyyyyy!" The voice came from outside. They both froze. "Heyyyy, Rickyyyyyyy!"

"That god damn nigga always turn up at the wrong time," Ricky said.

Houellebecq dropped the hammer and jumped when it struck the floor. "Who?"

"Neighbor guy always wearing a blue ass shirt. Don't worry, I'll take care of this nigga . . . God damn," Ricky said. "I hate that nigga!" He walked to the door and opened it a crack. A booming voice came into the room.

"Ay, Rick dog, I heard you in here, you back. Where you been, dog? I was worried you got picked up."

"I didn't get picked up, nigga, damn. Can't a nigga go away for a minute without everybody nosing in? What you want?"

"Come on, bro, sell me some and I'll smoke you up," the guy said, shoving the door and striding in. Sure enough, he was wearing a blue shirt. He had a big chest and a bigger stomach. He looked balder than Ricky remembered.

The guy took in the chunks of moldy drywall. "Whoa, you working on the place?"

The guy's eyes drifted to Houellebecq on the floor. "Who is this motherfucker?"

Houellebecq picked a lighter out of the rubble and lit a cigarette.

"You got company, bro?" the guy said.

"Just tell me how much you want so you can get the fuck out of here," Ricky said.

"Whoa, whoa, Rick. Here I stop by to patronize your local business when I already got some good shit set up while you were gone."

"Who?" Ricky said.

"Just some boys you ain't know," the guy said.

Ricky clicked his tongue. "Why the fuck you come here then, nigga?"

"Like I said, for your companionship. Now I want a quarter of an ounce for like, say, I got twenty on it."

"*Me cago en tu madre*," Ricky said. "I should ask you to get the fuck out of my establishment. I sell fire. You know this. And I sell it big. You can have an ounce for three hundred nigga. No, four hundred. For being like you is."

"Like I said, the guys across the street running a fine game. A quarter for thirty five."

Ricky looked at Houellebecq. He was watching with all the attention of a tired dog. "Can you believe this nigga?" Ricky said.

"I think I will try to sleep again. I feel as if I am bouncing inside my chest," Houellebecq said.

Ricky was feeling the same way.

"Is this some kind of faggot shit going on here?" the guy asked.

"Aite I got a new deal for you. You go out and score me some blows, a couple stamp bags, and I'll give you the quarter for thirty five."

"So I end up paying fifty five when I told you my final offer is thirty five. And that doesn't include the cost of labor."

Ricky raised the crowbar and put his face real close to the guy's. "Or I take the money from you right now."

"Whoa man, no need for violence. Aite, dog, you got a deal. I can just break even reselling after I take my half. Hear me? You're making me break even when I want a profit. I don't play that way, that shit ain't cool Ricky, and you ain't gonna hear from me again if you keep your prices like this and asking for whack ass junkie trades."

The guy left the basement and slammed the door. "So you have lost your number one customer," Houellebecq observed.

"Nah," Ricky said, "He always like that. Pretty sure he smoke it all himself, and pays by selling his mama's food stamps outside Aldi."

"Bro," Houellebecq said shyly. "What is a 'stamp bag'?

"A little something to make us chill out, maybe get some sleep."

"I am not an ignorant child—tell me what it is," Houellebecq said. "A barbiturate?" he asked hopefully.

"Naw it ain't a barbiturate nigga. It's blows. Opiates. H." Ricky said. "Aychhhhh."

A wonderfully strange and subversive enterprise
—*The Guardian*

Houellebecq had little interest in heroin. It was a drug for the most banal type of degenerates—suicide ideationists. They convince the world that their death drive is real by co-opting heroin's readymade images—the filth, the needles, the disease, the rockstar cut down in his prime, the used-up waif of a former model, the collapsed, nodding, drooling lump of human life, etc. Houellebecq considered it unimaginative to flirt with death in this way. Why not charm cobras? Why not venture into the forest and eat every plant in sight? Moreover, it was weak to float between life and death, unable to choose.

At this point, it did not matter what Houellebecq did or believed. With no cultural context or identity, in this basement with this oafish drug dealer, Houellebecq did not exist. What did exist were billions of flickering nerves inside a sweating body and an infernal, buzzing cloud of hornets in his head.

"I would like the heroin. I have enjoyed heroin in the past and I would like a particularly strong dose," Houellebecq said. He lied spontaneously without knowing why. Perhaps he could amuse himself by inventing fictions; this setting and relationship was uninteresting. A flash of humility made him think that it was arrogant to consider himself stronger than those who don't know whether they want to live or die.

"How much you like to bang?" Ricky said.

"A small spoon, filled totally."

Ricky smiled. "Huh," he said. "Aite, you'll get that much."

"Heyyyyyyy Ricky!" Ricky's atrocious "customer" was back. It had been less than an hour—Ricky wasn't lying when he said heroin was easy to get around here.

Ricky opened the drawer of the coffee table and took something out. He went to the door and cracked it open. "You get the stuff?"

"What? You not letting me in?" the customer said.

"Hell no. I ain't got time to fuck around with you today." Ricky held up a twisted up sandwich bag. "You want this or not?"

"Okay, okay, bro. Your girl finally up and leave your sorry ass or something?"

Ricky started to close the door. The man pushed it back. "Fuck, Rick. I got it," he said, digging in his pocket. He gave Ricky a handful of folded bills and small bags. "You acting like we ain't been bros for a minute."

"Aite man. See you." Ricky closed the door.

Ricky went to the kitchen and fiddled around in a drawer until he found a syringe and a spoon. Carefully tapping the powder out of both bags, he filled the spoon, which he took along with the syringe to Houellebecq. "There you go nigga, your small, totally-filled spoon. Bang that shit."

Houellebecq looked at the spoon and syringe. What exactly was required to transfer the powder to the syringe? Water? Spittle? Houellebecq remembered from movies that a flame was involved. He gave up pretending to know. "I prefer to snort my heroin," he said.

Ricky's head tilted back and he let out a long howl of laughter. He leaned back and laughed harder and harder until he was lying on the floor gasping for breath. "My nigga!" he said over and over. "My cheeks hurt." A couple more peels of laughter choked him. "You like to bang . . . a small ass spoon . . . filled totally, my nigga!" He caught his breath and grabbed the spoon. "Sit your ass up. I like to snort my heroin too. I only keep those syringes around in case a doper stops by and wants to buy a clean one." He took the spoon to the coffee table and dumped it out. "I ain't a seasoned junkie like you . . . Hehe," Ricky said. He used a scrap of paper to pull two tiny piles of the powder from the larger pile. "I only fuck with a tiny bit." He started giggling, then put his hand over his mouth and turned away from the table. "God damn, you gonna make me blow this powder all over the floor. So what you say, you want the other tiny bit I cut off for myself for later, or you gonna take down *all the rest?*"

Houellebecq couldn't help but to smile. It was refreshing to be teased. "I am just an old man trying to 'be cool.'"

"My nigga. It ain't like heroin's cool. Back in the day, I ain't never fuck with it." Ricky talked quietly while arranging the piles of powder in neat lines. "You here, that shit that happened with Elvia, writing books, chasing after you in Spain, that coffee joint, whatever the fuck's going on right now, it's like fuck it . . . whatever." With that, Ricky rolled the paper up, bent over the table, and inhaled the line of heroin. "Aah, shit," he said, handing the tube to Houellebecq. "You horn this. I'ma get some water or some shit."

Houellebecq took the rolled up piece of paper and held it to his nose. He remembered seeing Beigbeder's nose up against his silly silver cocaine straws. The coke was always a virgin white, like fresh snow, while this heroin was a snotty shade of yellow and brown. This is what belongs in a body such as mine, Houellebecq thought. He touched the straw to the line and inhaled as hard as he could. Houellebecq felt like the powder hit the back of his brain, which must have been connected to his sinuses because a bitter, medicinal syrup dripped down the back of his throat. His impulse was to swallow, but every time he did he felt like gagging.

Ricky popped open a can of soda and handed it to him. "Here, this helps," he said. "You didn't need to slam that shit so hard, I see your ass gagging. The dust supposed to coat the inside of your nose."

Houellebecq sipped the soda. Immediately he wanted to smoke a cigarette. He found himself offering one to Ricky; surprisingly, Ricky accepted. They smoked their cigarettes together in silence. The smoke swirled and rose slowly in the still air. Houellebecq sipped soda between every puff. The moment he finished his first cigarette, he lit another. These were the most amazing cigarettes of his life. Perhaps cigarettes, for all their pleasure, inherently caused a degree of pain, and this "painkiller" took that away, leaving only a sublime sensation. In cigarettes there existed heaven and hell—heroin washed away the hell. Houellebecq wanted to tell this to Ricky for some reason, but Ricky had started blabbing about literature again.

"I think now we'll be able to write some real shit. High niggas got the motivation to do anything. Sure, you heard of them niggas who suck dicks and steal TVs, but that ain't shit, man. I knew this nigga who'd been saving up to get a pound of pure. Course he was gonna sell a lot of it, but mostly it was to keep himself in dope, like a dope retirement plan and shit. Yo dog, can I get another smoke?"

Houellebecq shook one out of the pack and handed it over.

Ricky lit it. "So like, the nigga gets at the dude who sells the pure. They go to make the deal, some basic alley drive-up shit, but dude selling pulls a gun on homie, takes the money, and kicks him out the car. Now dude tries to drive off, but homie is like so pissed he gets his arms under the car and flips it right over, nigga. *Flips that shit right over.* Then he reaches through the window and grabs the dope off the ceiling of the car. After that, homie strolls off, kinda weighing the shit in his hand, while this hard nigga who came strapped is stuck in the car screaming like a bitch."

Houellebecq considered this story. "But that man did it for drugs. We are on drugs."

"Nigga! That's the part of the story you ain't think about. The guy was high. You think he ain't shoot up before he went to make the deal?"

Houellebecq considered reiterating that it was the desire for drugs, not the drugs themselves, that lent the man his superhuman strength. But he understood that the two were inseparable; in a sense, this was the question of the chicken or the egg. Furthermore, he was feeling good, almost even the oceanic feeling he had fantasized about so often in his books—so he chose, with deliberate delight, to believe Ricky's story. He wondered what writing on this stuff would be like. "Did you want to try writing now?" Houellebecq lit another cigarette. "Perhaps we can sit here side-by-side and write our respective books." He offered another cigarette to Ricky.

Ricky took the cigarette. "Oh, what, you ain't need 'total privacy' anymore, nigga? Haha. Come to think of it, I ain't want you peeping over my shoulder when

I'm writing a sexy bit about Elvia. That shit's private."

"I intend to watch over your shoulder and copy your writing verbatim. Perhaps I will translate it to French and I will win the Nobel this time." Houellebecq laughed and started coughing. He reached for the soda. "I have nothing to write."

"What was all them notes about then?"

"For a long time I planned to write about a genius urban planner. I have already written about a genius artist, a genius microbiologist, a genius comedian, a genius scientist, and, of course, myself, the genius writer. I thought an urban planner would be a simple addition to my oeuvre, but I have only a passing interest in the subject, and my interest in writing is constantly diminishing."

"An urban planner. Like a nigga that draws up new cities?"

"There are some new cities, but they are primarily in barbaric parts of Asia. Most urban planners reconceptualize already existing spaces, whether for governments or developers."

"So they'd never come up in the ghetto and mess around with it."

"They do not strictly mess with the ghetto, but they do determine the nature of public housing. The CHA buildings you showed me, for instance, are small townhomes. But at one time, it was thought that life would be more vibrant if each person was assigned an identical, strictly utilitarian space in a densely packed high rise building. I do not know that these kinds of housing projects were built in Chicago, but these boxy towers were built throughout the world beginning in the 60s. As this utopian vision faded, ideas like horizontal urban growth, for example with the suburbs, became popular, then later ideas like the repurposing of deprecated urban spaces, such as warehouses."

"But the shit around here was already kind of like those section eight buildings. Wouldn't an urban planner dream up some new shit for the ghetto, if he could bulldoze the whole thing beforehand?"

"Ah, but the problem with a ghetto in the first place is the people. If everybody here were made to leave and the buildings were to be repopulated through market forces, I am sure this would become a thriving community. There is no conceptual problem with this this neighborhood's layout."

Ricky stood up and fetched two sodas from the refrigerator. He cracked one open, took a sip, and let out a satisfied sigh. "The niggas who run shit in this neighborhood might like a little change in the layout. Like, giant fences and walls on every other block."

"What do you mean?"

"I mean, maybe this is stupid as fuck, but when you in the hood, you ain't got aldermen and neighborhood councils, you got gangs. A lot of them think of themselves as businessmen, and as businessmen, their only assets is territory. You can get guys, and you can get drugs, and you can get money, but you can only get that shit when you got blocks. And when you get the blocks, everything on them belong to you. That's why territory is really the only shit that anyone is willing to die for, I mean, beyond family and shit like that. See what I'm saying?"

Houellebecq lit another cigarette. "Certainly. The classic idea of borders."

Ricky lit another too. "Yeah. But it's more than that too, cause it ain't just the territory, but it's about keeping shit the same. Nobody ever want to sit down and say it, but the niggas in the hood hate change. You see a new nigga creeping around the block, and your first thought is that I'ma cap this nigga. But it's like that for everything, know what I mean? It's just like that coffee shop we went to . . . When they was first putting in shit like that, all the niggas around here kind of sat there and laughed at it, thought to themselves that these honkie ass yuppies gonna get themselves shot or mugged . . . But for the most part, ain't shit happen. Only shit that went on is some weird bullshit like teenager niggas popping out of an alley at 3 a.m. to hack at somebody's bike tire with a machete and scream 'get out our hood!'"

Classically xenophobic response, Houellebecq thought. Even 'hood niggas' can be reactionary nationalists.

Ricky went on. "Then a few years pass, and the white people kinda waltzing around, and now everybody just kind of scared. Half the hard niggas on this block are out west now, in the suburbs, and it's like, these were boys that would decapitate a nigga for stepping on the wrong corner, and the minute they see some skinny white bitch wearing yoga pants and walking a greyhound, they cross the street. It ain't like the gang leaders ain't see this . . . You think they don't sit around thinking about the days they ran shit on Damen and Huron? That shit's prime real estate—it was back when you could pull in twenty grand in a night on that corner, and it is now when you can sell twenty grand of some fancy ass coffee there in a day. Shit, nigga, sorry, I'm going on like I'm farting out my mouth," Ricky said. He looked at the empty soda can in his hand with shock, stood up, and fetched some more.

When Ricky returned Houellebecq offered him another cigarette. They smoked in silence. The drug was making Houellebecq's psoriasis act up. He lightly scratched his face, scared that if he continued he would scratch it raw.

Houellebecq said, "The gangsters, given the chance, would be more than happy to integrate with the quote white people. For example, the children of Arab immigrants, who should by all rights be armed militants, leap at the chance to work at offices and drink lattes in cafés. In fact, I saw some people who resembled you in that café today. One could chuckle at the fact that you and your Lilliputian computer were indeed there. Of course, those Arab childrens' parents probably owned small businesses. If the city were to give gangsters t-shirt shops and auto repair garages, in keeping with their entrepreneurial spirit, they themselves would become the enforcers of integration. The particular nastiness of the liberal system of culture is that it is perfectly transmissible. It is just as good for rich New Yorkers as it is for dirty Bangladeshis; if anything, the Bangladeshis are happier to have it, as I am sure would be the gangsters."

Ricky looked angry. "Fuck that," he said, lighting another cigarette. The pack was almost empty now. "You might be right. They might be happy with that. But it would rob them of the only real shit they got. They'd become the guy at the corner store, counting pennies and hollering at kids for stealing Twinkies, when they used to be soldiers, running like they on fire, pockets stuffed with bills with the heat on their tail, and the next intersection is somebody else's turf. Guys like that got love for life."

"Those men you know will be the last to die on that battlefield. The whole world is liberalizing. Their children will wither away behind fast food counters."

"Not if they stay the fuck away from the whites. How the whole world gonna 'liberalize' if I build those walls?"

The idea of building tiny walls all across the city that would actually impede people's movement was so patently stupid that Houellebecq didn't quite know how to respond. And yet . . . Isolated enclaves have always fascinated society at large. The existence of any given isolated population inevitably creates unprecedented worlds of culture, thought, and organization. The whole field of anthropology was based on this premise . . . China's Kowloon Walled City was a perfect contemporary analogy.

"You would create something similar to. . ." Houellebecq said hesitantly, "Innumerable Kowloon Walled Cities."

"The fuck?" Ricky said.

Houellebecq sighed. "I trust even your basic education included a mention of the Warsaw ghetto—"

"Naw," Ricky interrupted.

Houellebecq scowled and went on. "Kowloon was sort of like a Warsaw ghetto. Cut off from society at large, largely ungoverned, populated by people similar to one another. Illegal workshops and factories were created. Organized groups smuggled in food. A proprietary educational system arose. An entirely underground government formed, in Kowloon, controlled by the crime syndicates, in the Warsaw ghetto, by politically minded Jews, serving all the functions of the current state and new functions to meet the unique needs of the population. Perhaps an army would even assemble in each walled-off section." Houellebecq scratched his face furiously. "We need more cigarettes," he said.

"Let's hit up the store," Ricky said.

The pavement outside was damp. It was a misty night, and the sky was orange from city light trapped in low-hanging clouds. Houellebecq took a deep gulp of the fresh air then lit the last cigarette. "Allow me to clarify. You build tiny walls all over the city. The walls correspond to preexisting ethnic or cultural enclaves—let's call them spiritual boundaries. I am certain there is a particular neighborhood in Chicago that is densely populated by homosexuals, for example, and another for certain types of Asians. When a wall is built, these populations will instantly and fiercely protect it. They will begin to form the political and cultural life they desired, but found impossible to enact due to the need to conform with the political entity of the city. Imagine even the downtown area—the businesses and investors will immediately enlist the police, build the walls up to monstrous proportions, and create a sort of futuristic utopia for themselves, a small, ultra rich, vertically built technological megalopolis, replete with extensive tax shelters and unapologetically libertarian laws."

Ricky scratched his chin as they walked. "But you ain't want no one to get together. You ain't want mini-cities with mini-governments and shit. That's just more of the same. You want every man for himself. That way niggas live in fear."

"No community, no values, no identity, no society. Total isolation. Right. But there is no need to work out the specifics now. They should be worked out on the page. After all, this is an issue our characters will have to contend with."

"Yeah, yeah, so you down with the idea," Ricky said. "I know of a place they tearing something down. We can go get some bricks and get started building walls tonight," he said.

Houellebecq laughed. "No, my friend. What you can not do in real life, you do in literature." Houellebecq was a little ashamed of this poetic remark. He could not believe how nice he was feeling.

Ricky laughed too. "Aw, shit, yeah nigga, you right. I got excited and shit and forgot what we was even doing. Ha ha."

During the day Houellebecq hadn't noticed that the corner store's exterior was covered with neon lights. The store, glowing in the mist, could be seen from a block away. A beacon of possible Doritos, he thought.

"I gotta go in by myself because you a known con," Ricky said.

"Please get me a bag of Doritos."

"What kind?"

"Spicy Nachos, if they have it. Just not Cooler Ranch."

"You up on your Doritos game, nigga," Ricky said, chuckling. "I'll get you the cigarettes this time cause you been fronting me so many." He went inside and the door slammed with a jangle.

Houellebecq was alone for the first time since leaving Spain. He looked down the block at a group of blacks wearing red baseball caps and wondered what sort of thoughts about the city he'd have if he lived in a place like this. No throbbing bustle, no vertiginous speed, not even any noise. The tallest building in sight was two stories. Though it was brick, it had a set of garish vinyl-sided bay windows. They were peeling away from the facade as if they had been tacked on 100 years after the building had been built. Something like that defied rational critique. This was one of the few things that could make a poet lay down his pen.

The door jangled again and Ricky emerged with two packages of Newports, five bottles of soda, and a pouch of Cooler Ranch Doritos. "Sorry homie, they ain't have shit for Doritos here. If you went to the white grocery, you'd get like 10 flavors. Help me carry some this shit, that nigga in there wouldn't give me a bag cause of you."

Ricky shoved the Doritos into Houellebecq's arms and skulked down the sidewalk. Houellebecq lagged behind. He wasn't quite ready to go back inside. He felt like walking farther west, but at the same time he was excited that he may be able to go back and go straight to sleep. That would be heavenly.

Houellebecq found Ricky sitting on the couch and gripping his tiny laptop. "Ah yes, we were going to write," Houellebecq said. He sat down next to Ricky and thought about the idea of destroying liberalism through diminutive territorial divisions that lack community. The idea was shit, and Ricky was no writer. Ricky is a shit. The book will be shit. I am a shit, Houellebecq thought. He sighed with disappointment. But even while he sat defeated, he helplessly rummaged around in the thoughts of the evening, picking up pieces and connecting them until there was something worth writing down. It was just one line, but it could be the book's opening salvo. "No historian could have predicted that the city would be undoing the liberal-capitalist hegemonic system," Houellebecq muttered. Gaining confidence in his words, he loudly repeated the sentence. "No historian could have predicted that the city would be undoing the liberal-capitalist hegemony!"

Ricky nodded. "Yeah, yeah, yeah, yeah, good, good shit bro. You keep talking, I'll take it down." He pried open the laptop. "Repeat that?" Ricky listened carefully and typed.

"And nobody remembered Otto, one of the architects of cities, was the progenitor of the great undoing."

Ricky's tapping trailed off. "Hold up bro. Ain't no book I author gonna be about no fucking nigga named Otto. I thought this main bro was going to be from the hood."

"You can re-name him Manuel if you like. But he will be a Spaniard."

"Fine. But he a Spaniard who grew up on the West Side."

"Fine. Of Spain."

"Nigga, get the fuck on."

"All paths of human endeavor congregate and criss-cross in the city. Science, technology, art, mechanics, all of this could only rise to the greatest heights where the greatest minds met, themselves at the greatest heights. Newton said that men must stand on the shoulders of giants in order that they may see, yet even a giant could benefit by standing on the observation deck of a skyscraper." Houellebecq paused. "Cut that last line, that was a little joke."

"Aite, got it," Ricky said tapping hard, "But can you repeat the first part?"

"All paths of human endeavor criss-cross in the realm of urbanity. Science, art, mechanics—"

"Whoa," Ricky interrupted. "A, a, whoa, nigga. Mechanics? It ain't like I'm Mister Writer, but a mechanic works on a car. Buncha nigga mechanics criss-crossing out there on the streets? Hell no dog, my brother a mechanic, and he fat as fuck. I ain't never see him cross the street unless he in a car."

"Go ahead, delete it." Houellebecq realized with delight that he would soon be an author who wrote in multiple languages. He would be joining the likes of Beckett, Nabokov, and Joseph Conrad. Though the English in this book may be imperfect, people were bound to recognize the sophisticated ideas—some may even say genius—and find them all the more intriguing because of their imperfect expression. His legend would grow. He went so far as to consider writing a second book with Ricky, just so that Ricky could write it in Spanish. Such ludicrous optimism had to have been a direct product of the heroin he had snorted.

"Okay I got the next line," Ricky said. "It was December 2002."

"And?" Houellebecq asked.

"And the stars was bright."

Houellebecq laughed. "That is good but it does not go here. Save it." Houellebecq offered another line and Ricky wrote it down. Occasionally, Ricky added a line, and now and then Houellebecq included it, figuring that the reading public actually wants the sort of stupid, insipid, pandering, melodramatic shit that came naturally to Ricky. Together they hurtled and crashed through the world of words. They were somewhat like a buzzard with a parasitic twin attached at its belly—Houellebecq flitting above the expansive desert and periodically dive-bombing, and Ricky for the most part useless, but essential to the blood's circulation. They laid the bricks for their fictional city and created their character, a brilliant, aging drug dealer who "got out of the game" to practice urban planning. Partway through they took more heroin; all the while they smoked cigarettes and drank diet soda.

Houellebecq was dictating a long paragraph about the necessity of the transplantation of, or more accurately, the substitution of desires in order to delegitimize preexisting configurations of daily life, when he noticed that Ricky had stopped typing. Fast asleep, Ricky fell slowly over the armrest until his head hung from the end of the couch. The laptop slid out of his hands and bounced on the couch foam. Morning light was trickling through the block windows. The hunks of drywall and ripped splinters littering the floor came back to life. The basement had turned a weak blue.

Houellebecq looked at Ricky's face in this strange light and thought about Ricky's constant proclamation that they were "mobbing deep together now." Houellebecq had always thought that if he had been part of a more intelligent milieu, he would have been able to create better novels. Ricky, this basement, and the west side of Chicago yielded more intellectual fruit than the last twenty years of hobnobbing with European intelligentsia. The problem had been mediocrity. Shit was as good as gold; only copper was truly worthless.

None of this matters because this is a Novel of Ideas
—Bookforum

In the ensuing months, everything fell from Ricky's mind except Houellebecq, the novel, and heroin. Every day they woke up, took down a fat line, and got to work. "Scribbling," as Ricky liked to call it. Sometimes Houellebecq made weak instant coffee and complained about it. Ricky would tell him to carry his ass back to that coffee shop then. The two would continue sitting on the couch and letting the words flow.

Every Thursday morning when they tallied up their dope money—the meager profits of Ricky's remaining weed business—Ricky reassured himself that the book royalties would cover all these expenses and a lot more. He wondered if he'd even go on selling weed to that blue shirt nigga. He might just get himself a little place on the coast. Or he could throw the whole profits into investing in some real dope, a pound of pure, and build his business back up. He still had a few connections from the old days, and they'd be glad to hook him up again. Ricky constantly asked Houellebecq about the financial side of literature. "Yo dog, tell me again about how royalties work."

This was Houellebecq's shit. He loved to talk about it. "First the publisher gives you a sizeable advance. At least thirty thousand dollars. I have no idea how advances work when there are multiple authors, but I am sure each author receives a sizeable amount because that is only fair. Of course, the advance is counted against your royalties. But it is small in comparison. For every book that sells after the advance is taken up, you receive a couple dollars."

"Tell me again how many books you sold."

"Millions. Millions. But of course the money is not in books. It is meager in comparison to the film deals that Hollywood will offer us. See, here is where you being an American will help us out. The film industry buys book rights from known authors for millions of dollars—that is regardless of whether the film is made. Can you believe that! And if the film is made, it means more publicity. That translates to more book sales. The money never stops."

"I was in the wrong business," Ricky would solemnly say. And he'd feel grateful to this white geezer for sharing his knowledge and expertise. Ricky wondered if this was what having white friends was like. Hanging out with Houellebecq wasn't like sitting around with a bunch of hood niggas that ain't even know how to count on their own fingers.

The day they wrote the last line of the book, they had a hard time believing they were truly finished. They had sculpted a beautifully complex character. They had built a new city. They had tested the limits of human interaction. They had changed the fundamental way people lived. All on the page. Ricky read the final line aloud, savoring the sounds the words made, and the message. "And the human animal, deprived of other animals with which to hold congress, did its own thing for the first time."

Houellebecq smiled. Ricky said, after a pause, "Add in that when the animal did its own thing, ain't nobody see it and monkey-see-monkey-do, cause it was all alone."

"Unnecessary," Houellebecq said falteringly. When Houellebecq wasn't looking, Ricky added it in for good measure.

They were happy. But they both knew that would end with their final stamp bag. "Now we celebrate with our celebratory dope," Ricky said, pulling open the coffee table drawer. The last heroin baggie stared up at them with its green stamped mandela. Ricky tore it open, dumped it on the coffee table, and began assembling two fat-ass lines. In just three months their tolerance had reached what Ricky once would have considered a bullshit level.

"Just two boys with powdered noses," Houellebecq sang, snorting his line with gusto.

"Twwooooo boys," Ricky sang, taking down his line. "So how long before we rolling in dough?"

Houellebecq lit a cigarette. "My old publisher used to respond to me within the week. Of course, the book will be in your name and he will not know it is me, but it is still reasonable to expect a quick response, possibly two weeks, given the quality of this book."

"No doubt, no doubt. You know what I wanna do, my nigga?"

"What is it?"

"I wanna go outside and stare at the stars."

"We can go out . . . Stars for you, more cigarettes for me. I'll stop at the corner store. By the way, can you see stars from here? In Paris you cannot . . ."

The two walked along the block. For the first time they were free from thinking about the book, which made them think about it all the more. "You know," Houellebecq said. "The publisher would really get to the book more quickly if it was in my name."

"How we supposed to put it in your name though?"

"I had thought months ago when I first came here that if only I could issue a press release, or get in contact with the media, I could undo the slander that those people did to my name. Unfortunately I have neither an official website from which to issue a press release nor a trustworthy media contact."

"Dog, you wanna get the word out about sensitive shit nowadays, you use Wikileaks."

Houellebecq took a long drag from his cigarette. "Wikileaks. Ah, yes. I remember the controversy. It spoke to freedom. Well, my friend, I am feeling free today. What do you say?"

"Fuck it, let's go back and get the word out." They turned around and dashed back to the basement.

Inside, they both sniffed at the air. "You know, when you ain't making literature, you get to noticing that this place is damp and moldy as fuck," Ricky said.

"Yes. Funny that I only now notice it in earnest," Houellebecq said.

"Aite, let's get to it," Ricky said. He sat down, opened his laptop, and typed "Wiki" into Google. "There it is," Ricky said, clicking on Wikipedia. "How you spell your name again?"

"Give it to me," Houellebecq said, taking the laptop. He typed "Michel Houellebecq" into Wiki's search box and clicked his name. Houellebecq's date of birth, February 26, 1956, now had a dash and a date after it. "Unbelievable. I am staring at my own date of death." He scrolled to the death details. It was all there, the same shit Ricky had seen in the *New York Times* that day in the airport. Some sort of bombing, a writer lazily sleeping at 2:00 in the afternoon, the telltale dental record match. Houellebecq had later told Ricky something about having soft teeth.

"There you are, nigga! Now click edit," Ricky said. Houellebecq clicked it, quickly made sense of Wikipedia's markdown, and deleted all the mentions of his death as fast as he could, as if someone could stop his edit before he'd even published it. He clicked save. Trembling, they both stared at the screen. "Yeah, boy! You Wikileaked!"

They both lit cigarettes and smoked while they looked at the screen. "Hm . . . ," Houellebecq said. "But how can we be sure that some do-gooder will not believe the leak is false and change the page back?"

"Hm . . . If they do that, we change it back again. Show 'em what's good."

Ricky pulled a scale and a package of tiny Zip-loc baggies from a drawer in the coffee table. He was going to drop by the blue shirt nigga's house tomorrow and drop off a bunch of weed—his personal stash. Ever since starting on dope with Houellebecq, Ricky had lost interest in ganja. He wanted to spend the rest of the night dividing up his remaining weed. "It's value added when it comes pre-bagged," Ricky said. "Plus you can skimp." He and Houellebecq sat around weighing weed and putting together dime bags with less than a gram each. Ricky considered moistening the weed so that it'd feel a little heftier, but Houellebecq advised him against it.

．

The next day, Houellebecq's edit of his Wikipedia page was still standing. "We did it," they both said. They spent a couple hours putting the book into "manuscript form," which is what Houellebecq called adding page numbers and spaces between the lines. At the top of each page, it said "Houellebecq and Lopez." That was satisfying as fuck.

Houellebecq attached the manuscript to an email to his publisher and wrote a brief message.

> You will be surprised to know that I am still living (and writing.) I leaked this information on Wikipedia a day ago, so the media will be taking notice and redacting its lies soon. Enclosed is what may be my best work yet: a final and definitive roadmap to discredit the bases and structures of the liberal hegemonic system by creating regions of accelerated change. You will be delighted to know the book's principal language is English, and that it was written in collaboration with a member of the United States' revolutionary underclass.

"Underclass?" Ricky said. "Just because I live in this basement?"

"The word will sell. It is a code word that legitimizes your kind," Houellebecq assured him. He dropped a link to his Wikipedia page at the bottom of the message and hit send.

"Alright, nigga, we just got to wait for that reading bro to get his reading eyes over the whole thing. Meanwhile we got a handful of dime bags. I'ma come back with a handful of bills. We either get some dope with that, or it can cover one more shipment of weed. That's after setting aside money for smokes."

"I am confident our book will take care of us," Houellebecq said. "If not, we can always kill ourselves."

Ricky flashed a grin. "You right, nigga, I'ma get the dope." Ricky grabbed the dime bags and left, slamming the basement door. The blue shirt nigga lived across the street. It ain't like Ricky had to go past Homan. But still it was kind of freaky being out doing something that wasn't getting dope without Houellebecq. It was hot as fuck outside. As soon as the sun hit Ricky his shirt stuck to his chest. Guess that basement was keeping them cool all this time. Sort of like a tomb down there, Ricky thought. He hadn't noticed last summer cause he was either outside chilling the most or inside sweating like a bull while he fucked Elvia.

Ricky walked up the concrete steps to the blue shirt nigga's house. He tapped on the window beside the door, making those hollow rapping noises that were like a Bat Signal for drug dealers.

Ricky saw the curtain part. Then it fell back into place and he heard footsteps and locks clinking. "Rickyyyyyy," Jeremy called from inside. The door opened a smidgen. "To what do I have the pleasure of seeing you here?" Jeremy said loudly, poking his head out the door and looking up and down the block. "Get the fuck in here!" he whispered and dragged Ricky inside.

"You got the bud, my man?" Jeremy said.

"You got the money, my nigga?" Ricky said.

"Ah, dog, what's up with you?"

"What you mean?"

"First off, your face all puffy. Second, you uglier than usual. Thirdly, you smell weird. And finally, I bet you been doing blows. I been thinking about it since you asked me for 'em a couple months ago. What you want blows for? I been asking around, trying to figure out, 'What's Ricky want with that?' 'Does anybody know that old white boy in the basement?' You vanish for a couple months, call me out of the blue yesterday, and now you turn up looking turned out."

Jeremy's little girl peeked around his leg. "Daddy whatsa turned out?"

"You looking at it, baby," Jeremy said.

"Man, cut the bullshit and let's make the deal," Ricky said. "As we agreed on the phone. Or are you gonna make me renegotiate like always?"

Jeremy made a face and handed over a small stack of bills. Ricky carefully counted them and shoved the dime bags into Jeremy's chest. Ricky already had his hand on the doorknob when Jeremy said, "Hey, you finish up that work you were doing on your place? All that drywall and shit?"

Ricky stopped. "Drywall?"

"Man, all them holes you put in the wall. You installed new drywall, right?"

"Oh, oh yeah, nigga. Looks like Hollywood down there. Beautiful." Ricky kissed his fingers and opened the door. He went straight down the block to the dope guy and dropped all the cash Jeremy had given him. That was it for his money and possessions in the world, outside of the little computer he and Houellebecq had used to write the book. That was Ricky's little money-maker now. Ricky squeezed the stamp bags in his hand and traipsed back to Houellebecq. His mouth was watering in anticipation of railing a line.

"Ricky," Houellebecq practically shouted. "Red alert. The page was changed back!"

"What!?"

"I changed it again, but my edit didn't stay for more than a few minutes this time."

"Well change it back. Fast!" Ricky shouted.

"I am trying," Houellebecq said.

Ricky sat down next to Houellebecq and watched the screen. Ricky began to divide the dope into lines. "Don't worry, dog, we'll play it cool, keep watch over it tonight. If it won't stay true, we'll send the manuscript to your publisher again under my name."

"He will not like that at all," Houellebecq said. "That will confuse him, and he will think the whole thing is a hoax."

"Hoax or not, our book is the shit," Ricky said. He bent down and took his line. "Aw, fuck! Here you go, nigga."

Houellebecq hurried and slammed his line. He lit a cigarette. He edited the page again. He lit another cigarette and began to click refresh over and over. Eventually the page changed back to listing his death. "Fuck."

He clicked 'edit' for the sixth time, but now instead of pulling up the edit page, he was sent to a page that said he had been temporarily blocked from making changes. "What!" Houellebecq said. He navigated back to his page. Now a tiny padlock appeared in the corner where it used to say 'edit.'

They stewed silently and chain smoked. They had long since stopped buying soda—it cut into the dope money. Tap water was an unsatisfying replacement. They chugged it anyway.

"Man, it ain't no thing. We can submit it to other publishers and they'll take it, right?" Ricky said.

"Of course. But that will take months or years. Say we submit the book to ten other publishers. Half of them only read submissions from literary agents. My agent is dead. And we cannot acquire another one having no legitimacy or body of work. So we submit to the remaining five publishers. They all have strict submission periods, you cannot submit whenever you please. Then the book will end up in an intern's slush pile, where it will sit for months, perhaps endlessly, during the time that they call the 'reading period.' If they do read it and decide to accept it, they will request changes. That is all before it goes to design and manufacture, and of course they would expect us to have our own marketing plan. No, my publisher was our only hope."

"Can't we just print it up and spread it on the streets?"

Houellebecq laughed a bitter laugh. He looked like he could cry. "My bad, dog. I guess that was stupid," Ricky said.

"Yes, that was stupid."

They leaned back on the couch and continued smoking. Ricky looked at the layer of white powder that covered the coffee table. At the edges of the dope dust was ordinary dust. Ricky used to clean shit like that up, but now he sort of enjoyed the way he and Houellebecq left tracks in the filth. He especially enjoyed the accumulation of cigarette butts. Not a single piece of trash had been taken out of the basement in months, and if you took the time to really look, you could see thousands of cigarette butts in fast food cups and beer cans. Like bullets casings on a battlefield, Ricky thought.

Houellebecq suddenly stirred and put out his cigarette. "I just remembered something," he said. "This will be our *coup de grace*. Earlier this year, a friend told me about a new thing Amazon was doing using an online library to automatically generate reviews. Apparently the reviews were launching the careers of thousands of self-published authors.

"We laughed about it at the time. I remember looking at the automatic reviews for my books. They were not all that different from standard fare literary criticism, so I dismissed the excitement. But for those without a name, it would seem to represent the only chance of success."

"Why ain't we do that first, nigga?"

Houellebecq sighed. "Well, being published with a real publisher is like being signed to a record label for a musician. Self-publishing is like putting yourself on YouTube."

"But most new rappers get found through YouTube though. Like, the hot ones."

"I am not talking anymore. Now I am smoking," Houellebecq said, looking annoyed. Ricky decided not to get after him.

"Alright then, check it out. Just because we waiting on this doesn't mean we can't keep grinding. You know what Biggie said. Mo books, mo money. I got another idea," Ricky said.

"What is it, Ricky," Houellebecq said.

"Aite. So dig it. We go back to dawn-of-man days and shit. There's a big, black monkey in the jungle—"

Houellebecq made a sound like a mouse getting stomped.

"I'll get you some water." Ricky went to the kitchen and fiddled with the broken faucet. "So we in the jungle. Africa, wherever shit started. And this big, black monkey is stronger than the other bitch nigga monkeys. Better looking too. But he got a problem. Guess what it is though." Glass of water in each hand, Ricky turned from the sink and looked at Houellebecq on the couch. Houellebecq was cradling his head in his hands and leaning forward like he could fall on to the floor. "Sup, man. You ODing? Got a craving for an EpiPen?" Ricky said.

"At this point, our literary outputs need to diverge."

Ricky sat on the couch and tried to hand Houellebecq the water. Houellebecq didn't take it. Ricky set it on the coffee table. "We've got to diverge," he said. "What's that mean, you don't need me no more? You got a better idea than about the monkey?"

Houellebecq said nothing.

"That shit was half a joke anyway, but I thought it'd be kind of cool." Ricky paused. "Aite, if you don't want to write the next one with me that's cool. But does that mean we ain't writing together ever again?"

"My next book . . . ," Houellebecq began, "I can only think one book at a time. And for my next one, France's 'enfant terrible of literature,' that is, yours truly, hires a witch doctor to rip him from the mortal coil, and, back from the dead, a zombie, he exiles himself to Tibet—"

"Hold up, nigga," Ricky said. "What?"

"And, defying expectations, gets a position in healthcare, a hospital, and a 600-pound woman falls from her bed lift on him and severs his testicles, making him a eunuch . . ." Houellebecq babbled on. "Love and the erotic, for instance, will finally find a boundary, having achieved geomagnetic reversal, according to the galaxy's positions as outlined in the 1497 Gypsy's Almanac. I, personally, have been more influenced by the work of August Comte . . ."

Ricky noticed that Houellebecq had begun to weep. Was the dope or the moldy drywall making Houellebecq sick? They both fell asleep on the couch.

The period Houellebecq and Ricky spent waiting to hear from Houellebecq's publisher seemed to exist outside of time. They woke so late each day that they never saw natural light. The basement became more and more like a tomb, littered with artifacts from a long forgotten past: Ricky's small computer, Ricky's smashed bong, a refrigerator, fast food wrappers, Houellebecq's packet of identification papers, alcohol and coffee containers . . . Houellebecq and Ricky lay on the couch like mummies, wrapped in more or less the same clothes they'd worn from the airport. Ricky didn't bother killing 'danglers' anymore. In every corner, they wove delicate and perfect webs. Houellebecq's hair had grown back to the wild silvery nest he'd once been proud to comb out, but it was matted to his head. Thick cigarette smoke constantly swirled around their heads. The smoke felt like their savior—each puff briefly cut through the humidity that seemed to hang in the air like floating gelatin.

The only way to tell that the days passed was their dwindling supply of heroin and the curious change in their shared drug ritual. It used to be that as soon as Ricky and Houellebecq took their lines, they became animated and spoke unendingly about the ideas in the book, their futures, and what literature could accomplish. Now things were quick and quiet. The only thing worth talking about was when they'd do their next line of heroin, how much heroin they had left, how they might acquire more heroin, and the price and availability of heroin.

Houellebecq could barely recall his previous notions of the heroin addict's dance with death. He never could have imagined the profound joy of enslavement. And despite his poetic ideas about living a life dedicated totally and intensely to art, he didn't actually know until now what it was to want to die for something.

One day Ricky opened the computer and beckoned for Houellebecq to come look. Houellebecq knew it wouldn't be a response from the publisher. Houellebecq had suspected this day was coming ever since Ricky had conspiratorially asked him what a gutter was.

The Amazon page had nothing on it except a photograph that Ricky had apparently taken with the computer's webcam. It showed Houellebecq nodding off on the couch. The words "The Real Michel Houellebecq Still Alive" appeared on Houellebecq's torso in bright, sparkly letters. "I'm in the picture too," Ricky said. "You can see my hand there." He pointed to a corner of the photo where a hand flashing a gang sign could be seen.

Houellebecq restrained his anger. He had to give this a chance. Might as well take a look and see if it came out nice. He clicked the blue words that said 'Look Inside.' A mess of text littered the page. There were no paragraph breaks. He read a few lines and saw that a good deal of punctuation was missing. Scrolling forward, he saw that there were no page breaks or chapter headings. "Ricky," Houellebecq said, "how do you expect anyone to read this?"

"They ain't got to, only that computer algorithm got to read this. And a computer ain't gonna have trouble just going through to get a feel for the swag of the book." Ricky significantly lit a cigarette. "And I just published today. It said that review's gonna come rolling in tomorrow morning."

"Is it too late to take it down?"

"The fuck you talking about, nigga? We ain't heard back from your publisher. God knows we ain't gonna go through the trouble of sending it to those other publishers. This the only chance we got," Ricky said.

"I would rather publish nothing than associate my name with a flagrantly sloppy, pathetic abortion of a novel. This makes me ashamed," Houellebecq said.

"Hoo-hoo. Mister High and Mighty Houellebecq, the Capo Prince of Literature. Fuck outta here nigga." Ricky had a sour, hurt look on his face. Houellebecq knew it was useless talking more until that review was posted. "Trust me, dog. When this book starts selling we gonna be spending all our time stacking cash in a mansion somewhere. You'll get, like . . . Like, a whole writing wing to your own self. Think about that."

"Like I used to have. In Ireland. I had properties in Spain, France, and Ireland. And I had been thinking of buying in Thailand. I do not think we have understood each other all that well. We have understood one another only to the extent that two strangers crossing paths in a dense fog can recognize each other's forms as human and know not to take fright. Doing this with you has made me realize that my life should have come to an end long ago."

"The fuck does any of that mean? You think you're too good for me now?"

Houellebecq sighed. "No, Ricky." He lit a cigarette. "It is a simple accident that our destinies intertwined. Perhaps it was only possible because my destiny no longer had a form. The Buddhists assert that Nirvana is the same as a flame being snuffed out. Somehow the recent past has made me understand this more clearly."

"Whatever," Ricky said. He stomped off to the bedroom and, kicking a pile of clothing out of the way, shut the door. That was the first time that door had been closed since Houellebecq's first night in the basement.

> But even as Mr. Houellebecq embraces technology, he
> remains sceptical about how it may be used.
> —The Economist

Mr. Lopez,

Thank you, and at the same time no thank you, for sending *Minimalization through Urban Space*. We here at Flammarion Group do not usually write personalized rejections, but since we are sending you a cease-and-desist letter along with this rejection, we decided to include a brief note.

The cease-and-desist letter will outline the terms in which we ask you to refrain from all instances of using the late Michel Houellebecq's name or likeness to promote your own work. Additionally, I have referred your email to the police. I am certain that whatever you did to get Ernest's direct email was illegal.

Ernest asked me to read through your manuscript for legal purposes. I have to admit that I was intrigued to read an apparent parody of, or homage to, Houellebecq's work. What little amusement I expected to receive was entirely absent. This book is nothing but feeble minded pastiche. Though the idea is loosely reminiscent of something that may have been of interest to the late Michel Houellebecq, the tone is wrong and the characters are wrong. The work utterly lacks the intellectual rigor and sociological insights that lent Houellebecq his success. I say the words "wrong" and "lack," but those words suggest that this book aspired to something and fell short, which I do not believe is the case. The book is simply a mess. It is not even written in proper grammatical English.

Please do not take this personal response as an invitation to send more work. This work and all work of yours in the future is unconditionally rejected.

Irma Katzman

MINIMALIZATION THROUGH URBAN SPACE

Product Details
> Paperback: 322 pages
> Publisher: Ricky & Michel (July 24, 2014)
> Language: English
> ISBN-10: 0615594427
> ISBN-13: 978-0615594427
> Product Dimensions: 8 x 5.2 x 0.8 inches
> Shipping Weight: 15.5 ounces

Amazon LitCrit Review

It is said that early fame ruins careers. This phenomenon can be applied to literature regardless of time and geography. Take Kierkegaard. Kosinski. The late work of Tolstoy is terrible, as is, one might argue, the late work of Boccaccio. The particular vileness is usually achieved through the explosive mix of power, sentiment, and lack of inspiration. An author knows that he is read and studied, and therefore comes to believe that his fame can be used to advocate for his ideas. In short, famous authors become big idiots.

This is exactly the case with Michel Houellebecq, the *enfant terrible* of French literature who exited the literary scene several months ago. You would think that faking his death and stripping him of his worldly luxuries: bank account, mansions, societal connections, etc., would make him write something with emotional relevance and merit, perhaps something closer to his 1994 novel, *Extension du Domaine de la Lutte*, and farther from his 2013 novel, *La Carte et Le Territoire*. Instead, dear readers, it appears that an author, yanked from his soapbox of fame, will suffer from a Nietzsche-like degeneration of consciousness. This is what 2014's *Minimalization through Urban Space* has taught us.

An analysis of the language patterns used throughout the book shows that Houellebecq likely collaborated with an illiterate black American male. Such a collaboration could be fruitful if held to a rigid and careful structure. Instead, when it results in capitalization errors and randomly inserted slang terms, it tests the limits of readability. Obviously, experimental language has been used effectively by countless authors (Cummings, Joyce, Pierre Guyotat, Gertrude Stein, etc.), but you won't find any greater purpose here. You'll find only dripping sentiment, a stupid obsession with class politics, a college student's knowledge of urban planning and its implications, and a bizarre, almost mystical reverence of the institution of the family.

The characters are tired tropes and old retreads. Cross-referenced list of similar tropes has been deleted for length.

As for the theme, the idea of creating "zones of accelerated change" is a sloppy, haphazard, unattributed reproduction of an essay from a little known, possibly fictitious political theorist named Paul Treanor. If you have it in you to take this kind of idea seriously, you would do better to spend your time reading one of Treanor's actual tracts.

Houellebecq was capable of writing a true classic. We all expected him to eventually produce the most perfect art. This book is so profoundly bad that it may only be culturally significant as a pure reference to bad literature. To borrow the words of the authors, *Minimalization through Urban Space* is "raw dogshit."

•

Houellebecq read both texts twice during the time it took Ricky to read them once. When Ricky finally finished, he mouthed the words 'raw dogshit.'

"I know what you are going to say, Ricky," Houellebecq said, gazing off somewhere beyond the screen. "You are not black."

"C'mon, dog," Ricky said. "What am I supposed to say? I'm sorry?"

"The thing that sticks out to me is the fact that this review is completely unlike the other Amazon LitCrit reviews."

"What the fuck do that mean?" Ricky said.

"Ah . . . It is not perfect. It is sloppy. The paragraphs are not cohesive. It senselessly uses the first and second person perspective. LitCrit's other reviews have a sort of precision, or call it exhaustiveness, in addition to a delicate sense of authority. They would never call an author a big idiot, or even use the term 'idiot.' The LitCrit is known for making connections that weave into an irrefutable tapestry of the whole, not developing or in this case asserting testable theses . . . It is difficult to explain. I would have to show you," Houellebecq said, lunging for the computer.

Ricky stuck his arm out and pushed Houellebecq back. "Man, skip it. I ain't about to read another thousand pages on that dumb old screen."

"How did the LitCrit know I was alive . . . ," Houellebecq said quietly. He repeated himself louder. "How did it know I am alive!" He was furious.

"Relax, nigga. Ain't you remember Wikileaking? Shoot." Ricky guffawed. "And I listed you as the author on the page."

"No, you idiot. The review directly said that I had disappeared from the scene and forfeited my bank account and identity. It said I had faked my death, which is true in a sense, but we did not Wikileak any of those facts."

"Well it's a smart ass computer. It saw a new book with you listed as the writer, verified it was really you however the fuck they do that shit, and it figured all them facts out itself."

"That is not how computers work, damn it. It can only make use of preexisting information in a way that is has been programmed to. Computers do not—ah, God, if I have to explain artificial intelligence one more time . . . I cannot believe I am having this conversation with something real at stake. I should at least be high."

"Hold up, nigga, before you wild out and suck up the rest of our stash. What you trying to say?"

"Somehow . . . It sounds too crazy . . . But somehow I was set up."

Ricky let out one of his giant laughs. "HAHAHAHAHAHA! Nigga, you saying that like it's some unprecedented ass shit, like you Moses down on the rock or some shit nigga. But you figured that shit out the minute you got here. Come on, nigga, you ain't even remember how we talked about that bogus ass cop who gave you them fake IDs?"

"I know that, but I mean it differently this time. I mean, if you read this review in a certain light, it would seem that there was a conspiracy to strip me of my glory. To test me, to see if I would produce higher quality work if I were cast back down to the domain of struggle. That is, ordinary struggle."

"AHAHHAHAA! You on that X-Files tip now. You right, it's a conspiracy. Pretty much all of us a victim of the mastermind nigga in charge of making people who had something good fall to the bottom, lose their shit, and struggle just to live. Let me drop some wisdom on you, my guy. The world is wild and shit. Weird shit happen. But you can count on this, nigga: Shit roll downhill. And the world is nothing but a big old ball."

Houellebecq thought about that and got excited. It reminded him of the koan he'd been working on before he'd left Spain. "A ball whose rolling shit obeys the laws of gravity!" he exclaimed. "Rolling shit becomes a ball! A big enough ball forms its own gravitational field, Ricky! There is no up or downhill!"

"But what about pissing in the wind?"

"You do not do it."

"But I do."

"Ricky, fuck you and listen to me. The agent, or as you call him, 'bogus cop,' told me his name was Jack Reacher. That is our only clue for now."

"Jack Reacher . . . Nigga, I thought that smelled funky from the start. I swear I recognize that name. Let's type our little clue into Google and see if any registered police officers come up. Hehe."

The entire page was filled with results for a film starring Tom Cruise. "Yo nigga, since you met little homie, I got to ask you, is Tom Cruise as short as people say? I heard he a wild faggot too. He try to boogie with you?"

"Ah, Ricky, your good-natured teasing has a tendency to offend a nature as sensitive as mine."

"What."

"Do you want me to tell you that you were right all along?"

"Hell no, all I want is for you to enjoy this work of cinema." Ricky navigated an impossibly complex labyrinth of pop-up advertising pages until he reached a link that caused several tabs to open, each of which contained more advertisements. Somehow the movie began to play, although various ad jingles played over the orchestral music of the opening credits and introductory sequence.

Houellebecq and Ricky began watching in earnest when they saw the words "GET JACK REACHER" scrawled on a lined notepad.

"Who the hell is Jack Reacher?" the people in the film said. They did enough research to conclude that Jack Reacher was a ghost. No driver's license. No residence. No credit cards, no court history, no PO box, no cell phone.

"The man I met was merely using a pseudonym inspired by this film," Houellebecq said.

Tom Cruise appeared onscreen. Ricky pointed at him. "You mean this ain't your guy?"

They both lit cigarettes and focused on the action. People had been killed and somebody had done it. But things weren't what they seemed. A conspiracy was afoot.

Ricky started talking again about his monkey book. "It's like, this one ain't gonna be like your old books or any other old book. We talking about a fresh, crispy new scene. Primordial ass times."

"One moment," Houellebecq said. "Tom Cruise is describing a rape rally. I want to hear."

"Nigga, a rape rally's the only way we gonna get any puss with how much work we got to do."

"We will not do any more work. Shush," Houellebecq said. "I am enjoying the film."

"I ain't give a fuck about some wack white bro who iced a bunch of people. What I want to know is what we gonna do now. Rent being due and all, dope running out."

"Is that Werner Herzog?" Houellebecq said.

"Who the fuck?" Ricky said. "Warner Hog?"

"We asked you to clean up a mess, and you made another mess," Herzog said in the film.

"You know that nigga or something? Cause it seem like he speaking to us. All we doing is making messes out of messes," Ricky said. He broke into a fit of coughing. "Fuck, a nigga can't even breathe in this toxic ass dungeon."

"You could have cleaned it up at any point, Ricky . . . Now watch, this man is about to chew his own finger off . . . Ah! He could not do it! Of course not! I knew it. That character utterly lacks the required fortitude to do such a thing." Houellebecq said. He stuck a finger in his mouth and gnawed, wondering if he would be able to sever it to save his own life. Probably not, but perhaps if it were somebody else's life . . . ?

"Nigga, quit fucking around. This movie sucks. I like a movie like *Scarface*, you know, shit that you can understand. Scarface is a real nigga. Tom Cruise ain't even fuck that bitch even though the nigga showed his little-ass chest and the bitch was thirsty for it."

"Ricky, life is complicated. You do not always fuck the bitch."

"I would of fucked her," Ricky said. "Man, seeing Tom Cruise's swole ass made me realize I got flabby. Look at my titties, nigga. You waste your time finishing this movie, I'ma do some pull ups or something."

Houellebecq watched Ricky wander to the closet and dig around. "Fuck! Danglers all over this bitch!" he shouted, emerging with an over-the-door pull-up bar. Ricky batted at the bar with a balled-up plastic bag. Houellebecq returned his attention to the film.

Tom Cruise's character was becoming more important. He explained that nobody in the United States was truly free, if one were to consider anxiety a sort of shackle. A banal observation, Houellebecq thought, but pretty good for Tom Cruise.

Ricky was coughing and banging something around. Houellebecq looked up. Half the pull-up bar was wedged into the doorframe. Ricky was slamming the other end with his palm, and the wood frame was cracking and pulling away from the wall. It seemed unlikely that Ricky didn't know how to attach that bar.

"Are you mad, Ricky?" Houellebecq yelled. "Do you want me to come do pull ups with you?"

"Fuck you," Ricky shouted. "Watch your story. Big ass white Tom Cruise old face up in that screen."

Bang-bang-bang went the pull-up bar. Ricky groaned and sneezed. Houellebecq refused to look, to give Ricky the attention he so shamelessly craved. Ricky was clearly struggling with the world's complete and total rejection of their work, but Houellebecq wasn't about to comfort him. Every man suffers, but only the weak cannot cope on their own, Houellebecq thought.

Suddenly Ricky, the doorway, and the pull-up bar fell silent—Ricky clearly wasn't doing pull ups. Why did Herzog agree to play this ridiculous character, Houellebecq wondered, a German with a clear German accent playing a Russian who spent decades in Siberia? Why was Herzog playing any role whatsoever in a Tom Cruise movie? If Herzog heavily publicized his part in this film, he certainly damaged his reputation. Perhaps he thought that only American audiences would ever see this performance, so he had nothing to worry about. It delighted Houellebecq to think that Herzog may have taken Tom Cruise's money just to have taken money from

Tom Cruise. Or that Herzog got a profit-sharing agreement to take Tom Cruise's money for all time. Or, best of all, that Herzog realized the absurdity of the role and played it extravagantly just to make a mockery of the film. No one on set could have been the wiser—especially with Tom Cruise directing.

"You think I'm a hero? I am not a hero. I'm a drifter with nothing to lose," Tom Cruise said in the film.

"Nigga you a drifter," Ricky said. Then everything went black.

Houellebecq's last memory was Tom Cruise saying, "I mean to beat you to death and drink your blood from a boot."

•

Ricky looked at Houellebecq's body on the couch. It seemed shriveled and grey, like a dead bug in the corner, almost as if it had never been alive at all, except there was blood trickling from the wound on the forehead. Who could have known that you could dead this nigga with one hit from a pull-up bar, but flying to Spain and coming at the nigga with a hatchet, or strangling the nigga in an airport bathroom, wouldn't do shit.

Before fucking around with *pinche* Houellebecq, Ricky had been teaching himself to whistle. Now that the nigga was gone and Ricky was alone again, it seemed like a good time to practice. Ricky sat on the couch next to Houellebecq and pursed his lips. A single shrill, high pitched note escaped. Fuck! That still the only sound I can make, Ricky thought. Once a bitch, always a bitch.

He noticed that that bullshit ass Jack Reacher music had started up again from the laptop on the coffee table. The movie must have ended. Ricky haphazardly beat the laptop with the pull-up bar. It took a while to crush the screen and get the thing to shut up. It took even longer to pop a few keys off. Ricky picked up one of the keys and examined it. 'J.' J for joke, he thought. He whistled again, the same note. He held it as long as he could. I bet this note is a J note, he thought.

Ricky shoved Houellebecq's body aside and went to the kitchen. He opened the drawer and found his lone syringe. The last full stamp bag went into a little glass along with a splash of water. Ricky cooked it up and put it into a vein. He returned to the couch and dug around in the trash and rubble under the coffee table. When he found *The Elementary Particles*, he tucked it beneath Houellebecq's head.

It was 8 a.m. in Mountain View, California. The "Googleplex," Google's global headquarters, had not yet come to life. Most of the employees came in at 10 o'clock; the company had no formal attendance policy. If you came in early, you either had important work to do or you were a psycho.

One such psycho worked on the Books project. Every day he arrived at 7 a.m. and treasured the blissful three hours that were free from social interaction. During those hours, he browsed hockey box-scores, jerked off in the bathroom, and validated the data for one of Google's products, Google Reviews.

This was a long and tedious process that consisted of clicking around in a spreadsheet and making sure numbers looked 'right.' First he took a look at the number of reviews the Reviewer produced yesterday divided by the aggregate pagecount of the books reviewed. He compared that number to the same number for the last week, month, and year. Next he checked the web analytics and social metrics, first for the reviews on Google Books alone, then through Amazon's LitCrit, then combined. If a review received an unusual quantity of traffic, backlinks, or social shares, it populated in another column of the spreadsheet, which he could compare by day, month, and year. If a review generated an inordinate amount of user content in the form of comments, he reviewed the discourse and assigned a quality score, providing any comments he deemed necessary. Once a quarter, he met with his supervisors to review his findings; the results of that meeting would be passed along to the engineers who worked on the algorithms.

His final responsibility didn't have much to do with data. He was tasked with reading a few random reviews each day in order to find juicy content for the project newsletter. If a blurb was good enough, it might find its way to a humorous slide in a departmental meeting. Lately he'd been trawling the reviews for the self-published authors. He could usually find a delightful oddity, such as the Reviewer comparing a high schooler's gay werewolf erotica to Darwin's *The Formation of Vegetable Mould through the Action of Worms*.

Today he clicked into a review for a self-published book that was co-authored, which is usually a good sign of finding something deeply bad. *Minimalization through Urban Space*. Pretentious title, good, good, he thought. Pretty weird review. The Reviewer made some bizarre assertions about fame and artistic merit. Nothing much for the newsletter. But what's this stuff about an *"enfant terrible"* and an author faking his death . . . If this Houellebecq guy was some sort of famous author, what is this shitty self-published book doing on Amazon? he thought.

He did a quick Google search for 'Michel Houellebecq' and learned that the author had died earlier in the year. Ah, this was a problem. He leaned back in his chair, adjusted his sunglasses, and ran his hands along the front of his desk. Why didn't the program know that this author was dead? Could a simple impersonation on Amazon fool the program—if I published a book as James Joyce, would it think Joyce had come back to life? Seems like something I should report, but last time I reported that the Reviewer wasn't taking science fiction seriously enough, they told me that was fine and I shouldn't waste their time with shit like that.

He thought about notifying Amazon that somebody was self-publishing under a famous dead author's name, but he decided that that was Amazon's problem. He'd just correct the review on the backend. He'd already wasted enough time; he needed to hurry to the bathroom to jerk off before the herd arrived and all the dudes shuffled through to piss.

He clicked into the content management system, found the review, and changed all instances of 'Michel Houellebecq' to 'Ricky Lopez.' He shambled off to the bathroom.

Shafts of light bounced along the brightly painted doors and patterned rugs. Men and women of all ages and ethnicities strolled in with steaming cups of coffee. Managers smoothed their shirts, checked their watches, and hurried to meetings. Some of the younger men greeted each other and horsed around, shouting about television shows they'd watched the night before. Eco-conscious young women sat down at their desks and pulled on sweatshirts from their former Ivy League schools. These were the most brilliant men and women the world had to offer, and they had come to do cool things that matter. The whole office had a warm glow.